UP FROM THE MARSH

For Doug and Joan
Best wishes -
Affectionately,
Phyllis

Up from the Marsh

stories and poems

Phyllis Binkley

Fithian Press, McKinleyville, California · 2011

Printed in the United States of America

"A Convenient Place to Wait" was first published in *The Davidson Quarterly*.

Published by Fithian Press
A division of Daniel and Daniel, Publishers, Inc.
Post Office Box 2790
McKinleyville, CA 95519
www.danielpublishing.com

Distributed by SCB Distributors (800) 729-6423

LIBRARY OF CONGRESS CATALOGING-IN-PUBLICATION DATA
Binkley, Phyllis, (date)
Up from the marsh : stories and poems / by Phyllis Binkley.
p. cm.
ISBN 978-1-56474-512-5 (pbk. : alk. paper)
I. Title.
PS3615.I547U7 2011
813'.6--dc22
2010051826

The path through the marsh
disappears in the trees,
emerges under the clouds,
crosses the meadow, and
meets the roadways of mankind.

Contents

Of Our Time

Postscripts

UP FROM THE MARSH

"The Sisterhood"

BERT TOOK the unpaved county road across Eastpoint Heights instead of staying on Route One to Harbor Road. The washboard surface and occasional mudholes made the driving slow and rough, but she wanted this first look at the college by herself. When she reached the ridge above the harbor she turned off into the grass and stopped. To her right Gray's Inn sat solidly on the headland protecting the south side of the harbor, its stone walls seeming to grow straight up from the cliff below. Across the bay Eastpoint College stood similarly rooted in the rock of North Headland, its granite buildings breaking the long view of coves and promontories stretching along the coast to the north. From the ridge, the inn and college looked like twin fortresses, their domains extending inland to touch the high ground where it began to slant down to Eastpoint Harbor and the sea.

The air was clear, without a trace of haze, and the afternoon sun picked out every detail of the college buildings. Bertie could almost count the leaves in the ivy on North Tower, the slates on the roof of the library, the posts in the balustrade of the music terrace. She refocused, with an effort, as if she were changing a camera lens, and looked at the campus as a whole, miniaturizing it and making it remote. She pictured herself as she had been years ago, wholly contained in that cloister of familiar buildings and lawns and walkways. She had been more secure there than anywhere else before or since. Almost all of the happy times of her life, and hardly any unhappy ones, had happened at Eastpoint. Except in the best moments with Tom, and now in the precious hours with Bonnie, she had always had a sense of being away from the one place where she really belonged.

She wished now that she had come alone, that she hadn't asked the other six from North Tower to come. Too late for regrets now, she thought. Only pray that the weather holds for the weekend so we can get out and around. The forecast is bad.

Stupid of me to pick late summer, when we're likely to have a hurricane, or at best a dismal rain. She took one more long look at the college, and then started the car. She had to be on time. It was her party, after all.

Pez arrived at the inn first. After fifteen minutes, when no one else had come, she rummaged nervously through her purse for Bertie's letter and reread it quickly. She had the right date and place, all right; she was just early.

From the moment she had mailed her acceptance to Bertie she had been apprehensive about this gathering. The old certainty that she didn't belong, that they had only tolerated her out of kindness or good manners, was back as strong as ever. They had all been so bright and self-assured, with good clothes and enough money. She was the local girl on scholarship, one of the quota, Eastpointers said, that the college felt obliged to take from the farm and fishing families in town. She had been reminded of it every market day, when she could look down from the campus and watch the patched, rusty trucks coming in with potatoes for the produce depot. How many times had she come with her father in the old Ford pick-up, he in his worn dungarees, she in the starched jumper she always wore to call on the cousins in town. In that first year of college there had been many times when she had longed to go down and look for him, to ask him to take her home. She had never done it, knowing that he would have agreed, but would never have understood or forgiven her for throwing away her chance. In time she had learned to stop looking down on market days.

"Our little Polish doll," Rita used to call her. Pez had hated that. So had Hope, for some reason. She would say, "The only thing doll-like about Pez is that she's pretty." Hope was the only one of them who stood up to Rita. She herself had always felt intimidated by her, and it had been worse after she stole the money from the campus store. Clerking there hadn't really provided enough for books and clothes, but she had struggled along, with now and then a few dollars from her father. There had been dozens of times when she had found herself alone by the open cash drawer, but that one day, almost involuntarily, she had reached in and taken a packet of five-dollar bills. Within minutes she had regretted it and would have put it back if she could. But there was no chance. And when the theft was discovered she wasn't even questioned, because no one thought her capable of dishonesty.

If it had ended there, with nobody knowing, she might have been able to bury the memory, but that evening Rita had come into her room as she was stuffing the bills in the back of her desk drawer. Rita had said nothing, but the look on her face was enough. After that Pez had never been entirely free from her shame, although she had managed, in fifteen years, to thrust it deeper into her mind, so that it haunted her less.

She wondered why, of all the memories she could have brought up, the least welcome ones should pop to the surface unbidden. To make things worse, she was beginning to tremble. She found a chair in the lobby and sat down. This is foolish, she told herself, you're equal now. A degree with honors, a successful career, then a good husband and a happy family. Just the thought of Peter comforted her. Old-fashioned and loving, he was dependable, as her father had been.

She felt even better when Jan came through the foyer, caught sight of her, and smiled, a wholehearted smile of gladness. Pez rose and Jan took her hand, then put one arm around her shoulders.

"Pez, you look wonderful—not a bit older."

Pez blushed. She knew it was true, but she thought it was about time she began to look her age. Jan did. Her face was thinner, her eyes deeper somehow, and her forehead had faint lines.

"I'm glad to see you, Jan. I was beginning to think no one else would show up."

"Dear Pez, still our chief worrier. I gather you're the first. Do you know if Hope's coming?"

The smile on Pez's face diminished. Jan cursed herself. Clumsily, she had made Pez feel less special. Worse, she had revealed too much, given herself away. After fifteen years, I'm out of practice in deception. Luckily it was only Pez. She intensified her smile and added, "It's just that the last I knew, she was the only one Bertie hadn't heard from."

Pez seemed soothed. "Oh, I think she'll come. Bertie wrote me that everyone would be here. Look, there's Bertie now, and Rita."

"Bertie looks as fit as she did in school," Jan commented. "But I suppose athletic directors have to. And Rita's just as elegant as ever."

Uncertainty gave way to awkward hugs and a jumble of greetings. "Did you grow some more after college, Bertie?" "No, honey, I think everyone else shrank." "I see you've been nominated to the Appellate Court, Rita. Congratulations." "Not yet, Jan, I haven't been confirmed." "Pezzie, it's unfair. You haven't changed a bit." Pez blushed again, and Jan thought she would probably stay that color the entire weekend.

Hope came at the same time as Agnes and Ruth. Jan looked up in response to Rita's "Here's the rest of the gang," her gaze touched Hope's, and for a moment she felt paralyzed. There was another round of simultaneous talking and hugging, during which Hope came over and touched her cheek to Jan's. "Hello, Jan, you look well."

"You, too," Jan said. Her heart was pounding and she knew all the color had left her face. She was grateful for the hubbub around them.

"I never thought we'd really do it," Agnes was saying. "Fifteen years. I don't believe it."

Hope said, "What I don't believe is that we're still all recognizable. At least you all are. I don't know about me."

"You are," Pez said, "but thinner. Like Jan."

Jan found her voice. "Yes, you are. It's becoming."

"Don't tell me you two haven't seen each other since graduation," Rita said. "Of all of us, I would have thought. . . ." She left the sentence unfinished. Jan had forgotten Rita's gift for insinuation.

"Nope. Too busy raising families, I guess." Hope's voice was casual, and she didn't look at Jan.

After that it was easier. They all moved toward the desk, where Bertie took charge. "I didn't have time to check with everyone about rooms," she said, "so I just took a chance. They had two doubles with baths and across the hall a suite for three with bath. I thought Jan and Hope might like to be roommates again, and I paired Rita with me, leaving the triple for Pez and Ruth and Agnes. Is that okay?"

Jan made her voice light. "If I could stand it for four years I guess four days is no problem. How about it, Hope?"

"Why not? You haven't started to snore, have you?" Hope's drawl had always been more pronounced when she was working at casualness. How quickly we've resumed our camouflage, Jan thought.

"How about the rest of you?" Bert asked.

"Fine with me," Rita said, with that hint of irony that had always seemed to say, I'll go along but I would have done it differently myself. She added, "But I worry about Ruth. How is she going to get a word in, with Pez and Aggie chattering away?"

Everyone laughed, including Pez and Agnes. Pez said, "It isn't that Aggie and I talk a lot; it's just that Ruth's so quiet."

Ruth smiled. "Maybe not so much now. Remember, I was new in this country then. North Tower was an amazement, such a busy, noisy, hurrying place. It seemed that you never walked, you ran. And you spoke so fast. I had good English, I thought, but I was always two sentences behind."

"I'm sure you thought we were nothing but a bunch of silly American schoolgirls," Rita said. Jan winced. The comment was so unnecessary, begging as it did for denial. Another thing she had forgotten was that Rita's usually controlled sense of superiority could occasionally get out of hand, creating small embarrassments like this. She wondered if Ruth, who was kind, would make the expected reply.

"I didn't say that." There was a hint of sharpness, quickly softened as Ruth added, "Actually, I was a little in awe of you."

Jan was surprised. Worldly Ruth, who had been born in Brussels and had grown up in London, who had gone to exclusive private schools in Zurich and Rome, who had a better education than any of them could even aspire to. She had thought that Ruth's quiet smile covered amusement at their naiveté, and she said so now.

"No, that must have been a nervous smile. But I'm sorry you thought I would laugh at you. I must have seemed very condescending."

"Never," said Hope. "Condescension was Rita's thing. She had it down to a fine art. Didn't you, Rita?"

If someone had picked up the vase of flowers on the desk and thrown it against the wall, the shock would not have been greater. Jan was appalled. Hope had always been blunt, but this was unnecessary. Rita had turned pale, and there was deep anger in her eyes.

"Don't be offended," Hope went on. "No one had a better right. Head of the class, Phi Beta Kappa, student president, first-class athlete. The rest of us, with our human frailties and academic shortcomings, couldn't hold a candle. I don't think you even knew how patronizing you were sometimes. Just sometimes, Rita. It was tolerable."

The barb had been withdrawn with barely a speck of blood shed. Someone let out an enormous sigh and Jan realized it was Pez, who looked as if she had been about to cry.

"All right, Quickdraw," Bertie said to Hope. "Check your weapon at the desk. This gathering's going to stay peaceful."

Score a big point for Bertie, Jan thought. Hope smiled, Rita smiled, and everyone began talking again.

Later, while they were unpacking, Jan said to Hope, "That was uncalled for. Why did you do it?"

"She was being so snide. First that sly dig at us, then the crack about Aggie and Pez, then twisting Ruth's words into that 'silly schoolgirls' remark."

"Ruth took care of that very neatly herself. And Pez and Aggie laughed right along with the rest of us. As for the other—well, she was right, wasn't she? You can't blame Rita because we weren't always clever enough to hide our feelings."

Hope looked at her soberly. "I'm not. But she's so maliciously virtuous. She hasn't got an ounce of understanding. She makes what we feel—felt—seem degrading and pitiable. How does she know how other people feel, how they are with each other?"

"Maybe," Jan said, struggling for the right words, "she does know. Maybe she recognizes things in the rest of us because she senses them in herself. The old business that it takes one to know one. And then, well, maybe a spiteful tongue bespeaks a jealous heart." She was surprised at herself. "Now I'm the one passing judgement."

Hope smiled. "You're too wise. And right that I shouldn't have jumped all over her. I'm sorry. Now let's go to dinner, and I'll be sweet as pie to everyone."

Dinner turned into a concerted effort to mollify and praise Rita. Ruth looked around the table and thought it might as well have been rectangular, with Rita at the head, she was so clearly the center of attention. Bertie began by raising her wineglass. "Here's to our about-to-be judge. Long years and many future successes." Rita replied modestly, saying that she wasn't going to be fitted for a robe until she was confirmed. "Besides, this was one of those lucky breaks. I don't think a man of my age would have been appointed. They were looking for a woman and I happened to have the right experience."

Ruth admired her honest evaluation, but was not persuaded that the modesty was entirely genuine. She glanced at Hope to see her reaction, and caught her looking at Jan, who was staring at her plate. Those two, Ruth thought, still believing they had been guilty of a desperate sin. They should have gone to school in Europe. She caught herself: Here I am after all, laughing a little at Americans. But they do set such inflexible standards in some things and are so undisciplined in others.

"Do you remember the day we put the goat in the elevator?" Bertie asked Rita. It was the first "do-you-remember" and Ruth thought it remarkable that it had taken so long.

"We?" said Rita. "As I recall, you were leading it and Agnes was pushing."

"Yes, but you and Jan were look-outs, and the only reason the others weren't helping was because they were laughing so hard."

"At me," Ruth said, "because I'd stepped in the goat's indiscretion."

"Indiscretion!" Hope's laughter spilled out uncontrollably and continued until tears ran down her face. The others laughed at her laughter, and soon people began to look over and smile with them. A white-haired man at the next table leaned over and said, "I once dragged a cow into my faculty advisor's office. By the time they found it, they had a whole wheelbarrow of indiscretion to shovel up."

This set them off again, and dinner ended with a party in the bar which included the white-haired man and his family, and half a dozen others. The man was an Eastpoint alumnus, and when they explained to him that they had shared the North Tower section of the women's dormitory during their undergraduate years, he said, "You know what we called North Tower back in my day? The nunnery."

Unexpectedly, it was Agnes who said, with the smallest of smiles, "that would have been less appropriate in our time." Everyone laughed, but Ruth saw that Jan and Hope were looking at Agnes anxiously. She went on: "A sisterhood, maybe. A sisterhood by chance. But the resemblance to a nunnery stopped there."

"Oh, I don't know," Hope said. "Rita was a darned good mother superior."

Ruth thought Rita might bristle again, but apparently the wine had muted her sensitivity, for she smiled and let it pass.

On their way upstairs, Ruth contrived to walk with Hope. "Don't be too hard on Rita," she said. "She must be understood, too, even if it's not so easy as with the rest."

"I hope the weather holds," Rita said to Bertie as she came out of the bathroom. "It'll be hard to keep up the camaraderie if we have to sit around indoors looking at each other for three long days."

"Don't worry," Bertie said. "If worst comes to worst we can go over to the college library and pretend we're back cramming for exams." She stopped abruptly and picked up her hairbrush. After a dozen fierce pulls through thick, curly, now graying hair, she resumed talking. The lightness was gone from her voice, and her words came painfully. "Speaking of exams, I owe you, don't I? For not reporting me on that political science final. I never had a chance to talk to you about it, with commencement and all."

"Forget it. It wasn't important." Rita had not intended to sound so harsh.

"Yes it was. It still bothers me. By rights I shouldn't be here. I don't know why you let it go. It wasn't like you."

"It wasn't like you to cheat. I couldn't have hurt you that much." That had been the smallest part of the reason, Rita knew, if it had in truth been any part. The plain fact was that the consequences for herself would have been too unpleasant. She had recognized even then that popular morality does not subscribe to higher, more demanding principles. How many times did I bend those principles, she wondered. With Pez, with Agnes, with Jan and Hope. It wasn't caring, or forgiveness, at all. But she knew better than to explain that to them. They wouldn't have understood, then or now.

Bertie was looking at her oddly. Rita hoped her thoughts hadn't shown in her face. She said, "It was a long time ago. You should forget it."

"I'll never be able to," Bertie answered. "I had no business taking that course. I guess I was trying to prove something. It turned out I did—that I was neither as bright or as honest as I thought. Anyway, thanks."

From across the way they could hear the amiable chatter of Agnes and Pez, with occasional comments from Ruth, and next door the low, steady voices of Jan and Hope. I don't belong here, Rita thought, with these people I left behind fifteen years ago. If we ever had anything in common we don't now. I can't even think of what to say to poor old Bert. She should be in there with the others.

"Listen to them," Bertie said. "If this keeps up they'll all be sacked out until noon. Maybe we should've set a curfew."

The storm began during the night, first with brief, tentative showers patting the leaves, then intensifying to a steady hammering on the roof that reminded Agnes of her childhood on the ranch. Nothing in that childhood had prepared her for moving into a wider world, and she had never been so relieved as when Malcolm, whom she had grown up with, came with her parents to her commencement, with an engagement ring in his pocket. The years at Eastpoint had receded as she fit herself into the quiet duties and pleasures of a country woman. Malcolm might boast about his wife's keen handling of the ranch accounts, her importance on the county agriculture committee, and her work with church and youth groups, but it was her family and gardens that brought her the greatest contentment. Especially the children.

She wondered why she had come to this reunion. For all of the happy times at North Tower, her college days had only one real memory, still so horrifying that she could not force herself to relive it from start to finish, all in one piece. A small incident might recall Ralph standing in the lab, his eyes seeming to undress her in front of everyone, but her mind would not go on to the seduction that followed. Each of her pregnancies had brought shattering recollections of the day at Eastpoint she had realized she was going to have a baby, but she would shut out the night that Ralph had rejected her. When her children persisted in transparent lies, or refused to accept painful realities, her anguish for them recalled her own refusal to admit the pregnancy, to do anything about it other than to conceal it every way she could. And in each later childbirth she had recalled the grim night when she had crawled to the bathroom and tried to deliver the baby by herself, then recovering consciousness to find Hope holding her and Jan bundling the dead infant and afterbirth in towels and sheets. Both of them, pale and uncertain, cleaning up and comforting her. "Someone, we think Rita, opened the door right after we got here, but whoever it was never came in," Hope had said. "I think we're the only ones who know." They had taken her to a town doctor twice, but other than that they had never referred to it, had never treated her any differently than they had before, except for a special protectiveness that had often brought her close to tears.

She supposed that was why she had come for this weekend, to see Jan and Hope, to show them she had made it, that the scar had almost disappeared.

The rain was having its usual effect on her. Ruth's and Pez's deep, even breathing added to her sleepiness. She thought how nice it was that Jan and Hope had each married happily. They had been too dependent on each other back then.

❧

Hope was sure that Jan was still awake too, but as she had so many times in the years in North Tower, she lay still and said nothing. It was totally unexpected, the reawakening of those feelings that she had long since explained away as just a phase of their youth. She recalled clearly, as she had not done since the first years after their parting, the few times when neither one of them had been strong enough to resist the need to touch. She was as shaken and confused now as she had been by those tender, awkward encounters years ago.

The rainstorm had grown fiercer and the blanket and spread at the foot of her bed began to feel damp. She explored with her feet. The coverings were soaked.

"For Pete's sake," she muttered. Kneeling in the middle of the bed, she put out her hands to see if she could locate the source of the water. There was a steady drip from the ceiling. Trying not to make any noise, she climbed out and began to inch the bed cautiously out from under the leak.

"What on earth are you doing?" Jan turned on the light.

"Sorry. The damn roof's leaking on my bed."

"Here, let me help."

Together they lifted the bed out of the way. Jan put a tin wastebasket under the leak. The metallic ding of the water dripping into the basket set them both to giggling. Hope went to the bathroom for towels, put one under the basket, and draped another over it loosely.

"Rita and Bertie are probably wondering what all the clatter is," Hope said. "It must sound very odd."

"I'm sure Rita thinks she's got it all figured out."

Hope went to the other side of the room, putting as much distance as she could between Jan and herself. "I have to tell you," she said, "that if it were up to me she'd be right. I never thought this would happen. We're thirty-five years old, happily married, with children. It's ridiculous."

"Yes. Even my heartbeat's gone adolescent on me. If it doesn't slow down I'll be a stretcher case." Jan was smiling in a different way now. "I've been thinking about it, lying in bed just now. Is it wrong, morally, the way we always thought it was, or is it something that just happens sometimes, something natural and acceptable? The rules seem to be changing."

"Did you ever talk about it with your husband?"

"No. You?"

"No." Hope thought about it. "You know, I don't think he'd be shocked. Brian's a very understanding guy."

"So's Dick," Jan said. "The four of us should get together sometime."

The moment had passed, Hope thought, and they were on high ground. "I'm going to bed and get some sleep. Heaven knows what Bertie has planned for tomorrow, but I bet it's something athletic, rain or not."

"Is your bed dry enough?"

"Yes," Hope said firmly. She crawled in and turned off the light. "If nothing else, it's nice to know it wasn't superficial. It lasted. That makes it important, doesn't it?"

"Yes," Jan said. "Good night."

Friday produced a misty drizzle, dampening but light enough to allow Ruth and Bertie several games of tennis, and Rita, Pez, Jan, and Hope nine holes of golf. Agnes watched the tennis for a while, then wandered off toward the gardens that surrounded the inn. The vegetable garden was larger than her own, at least half of it devoted to what she thought of as salad vegetables. She was especially impressed with the celery. She'd never had much luck with celery. Absentmindedly, she bent down and began weeding.

"We don't get many guests who weed the gardens for recreation." It was the innkeeper, a robust man, bald on top but otherwise covered with reddish-blond hair so thick it resembled fur. He looks like the pirate in the old comic strip, Agnes thought.

"I'm sorry," she said. "I didn't mean to be nervy. It was habit, I guess. See a weed, pull it up. The bad ones, at least."

"All weeds are bad as far as I'm concerned."

"Oh, no. Some are so pretty. Those Michaelmas daisies, do you see, and the mullein and Queen Anne's lace." Agnes saw that the innkeeper was as uncomprehending as Malcolm when it came to her convictions about weeds. She dropped the subject.

"You're one of the seven ladies who checked in yesterday, aren't you?"

"That's right." The way he said ladies was obscurely pleasing.

"I noticed in the register that you're all from different places. What brings you here?"

The question seemed intrusive, and not prompted by any real interest, but perhaps he thought an innkeeper had to conduct little chats like this with his patrons. Maybe it came from a course in hotel administration. She answered briefly, trying not to seem rude. "We were classmates at the college years ago."

"Wonderful." He was far more enthusiastic than he had to be, as if it was the first gathering of its kind he had ever witnessed. "Reliving the old days, hey?"

"Something like that." What had prompted them all to agree to this? Certainly not to relive college memories, except maybe Bertie. Agnes thought she knew why she herself had come, but why the others? Partly curiosity, she was sure, but there had to be more than that. It could be a need to refresh perspectives on people who once were closer than family and now were so remote. But why should any of us care, even if we were to lose touch altogether?

"—beer parties and football games," the innkeeper was saying. She had missed his point, but she thought a polite smile would do for a reply. Then she excused herself and moved away, toward Jan and Hope, who were coming down the road from the golf course.

"Hi. How was it?"

"Wet," Hope said. "We all played badly except Pez. She had an eagle on one hole and birdied two others. It turns out that she plays with her husband all the time."

"That should put her inferiority feelings to rest for a while," Agnes said.

"I hope so," Jan said. "Even Rita was impressed. For once she couldn't put Pez down. Pez will be glowing for the rest of the day. What have you been up to, Aggie?"

"For a while I watched Bertie and Ruth working themselves into a sweat, then I wandered in the gardens. I met the owner. He's one of those awfully genial hosts, very chatty." She made a face.

Jan and Hope laughed. "That's not like you, Aggie," Hope said.

"No, it isn't," Agnes conceded. "He wanted to know what had brought us all together here. I resented the question, I don't know why. It was too personal. I only half know why I came, and I certainly couldn't answer for anyone else."

"I wonder myself," Jan said. She looked first at Hope, then at Agnes, looks so openly loving that Agnes found it impossible to breathe for a moment. Hope stood completely still. Jan added, "Whatever the reason, I'm glad I came." She put an arm around each of them and they began walking back towards the inn. "Why did you come, Agnes?"

"More than anything, I guess, I wanted to see you two. To tell you that everything has been fine. I've never forgotten—"

"You should. As much as you can." Hope's voice was soft, almost inaudible.

Because Hope was usually brusque, Agnes was even more moved by her gentleness than by Jan's. "I wish I could see more of you two," she said.

"I wonder. Everyone will be saying that all weekend, but I wonder," Hope said.

By five o'clock the continuing dreary weather had begun to take its toll. Even Bertie's enthusiasm was faltering. The afternoon had dragged for all but Ruth, who had spent most of it playing the piano in one of the small parlors on the main floor. She had only recently begun playing again, and she deeply regretted that she had ever stopped. The profound concentration needed, first to reacquire the dexterity she had lost and then to master each new piece of music, pushed out every other concern of her life. Most of all it temporarily dispelled the deep homesickness that had grown stronger each year she had spent in America. By now, she thought, this country should be my home. I've been here longer than in any other place. But compared to the cities of Europe, Boston where she had lived after college, and New York where she had moved after marriage, were harsh landscapes, inhabited by harsh people. Moving to Westchester may have benefited the rest of her family but it had made her feel even more isolated. She loved her children but did not feel she could compromise as she would have to, in order to become a suburban mother. She had not joined the parent-teacher group, had not become a scout leader, had not done a host of other things everyone seemed to think she should. She wanted her children to develop themselves each in accordance with the talents God had given them, and it quite literally grieved her to see them becoming homogenized.

Perhaps, she thought, the reason I'm here right now is to try to fall in love with this country again, as I did at first. These girls took me in so matter-of-factly, so warmly. If I had expressed my gratitude, they would have been surprised. No big deal, they would have said.

Someone sat down next to her on the piano bench. She was briefly annoyed, then saw it was Bertie.

"That's the Mozart C-Minor Fantasy, isn't it?"

"After a fashion, yes. I'm still trying to get this fast allegro part right. But I didn't know you knew classical music, Bertie. Do you play?"

"A little. Not well. Even if I practiced every day, I couldn't touch you—no feeling for it. But I like to play. Simple things."

Bertie watched Ruth's hands, how lightly they moved. Her own fingers seemed to plod, and no amount of determination could make them nimble. The story of my life, she thought. Everything comes slow and hard. Even in sports, my own field, I'm not first-rate. I don't know why I got all gung-ho about this reunion. They make me feel so unexceptional. Yet I love being with them. Together we were such a good group. Even Rita fit in, thought she might not think so. She tried to put aside her worry that this weekend might not be the success she wanted it to be. She said a short silent prayer for an improvement in the weather.

"I think I've got a great idea," she said to Ruth. "Why don't we have our before-dinner drinks in here and sing? Would you play for us?"

Ruth suppressed an urge to say no. She didn't care for popular music at all. "Only if you promise it won't be one of those affairs where everyone sings the old college songs and goes all maudlin."

"With this group? There isn't a Maud among us." Bertie looked pleased at her word play. "Not bad for a phys-ed major, hey? I'll go round them up."

It was an unenthusiastic group at first. Then Pez asked shyly if Ruth knew "Danny Boy." They all joined in dutifully when Ruth began to play, but as Pez's clear soprano gained strength they stopped, one by one. She sang two verses before she realized she was singing alone, and her voice trailed off.

"That was lovely, Pez," Jan said. "Go on."

Flustered, Pez declined. "It's someone else's turn."

There was a clamor for her to go on, but Pez, red-faced, refused. Hope came to her rescue. "Jan and I double-dated for a while with a couple of TKE's. They sang the best songs at their parties—"

"Careful," Rita warned.

"Clean songs," Hope insisted. "Well, a lot of them. Do you know 'You Can't Get to Heaven,' Ruth?"

"I don't think so."

"We'll sing it. You can pick it up. Come on, Jan."

Not entirely tuneful, but lively, Hope's and Jan's effort inspired the rest. Rounds, improvisations, camp songs followed one after another. The white-haired man and several others drifted in and the innkeeper, delighted to see his dispirited flock enjoying themselves in spite of their indoor confinement, served a free round of drinks.

Bertie beamed at Ruth. "Thank God for you," she said. "You saved the day."

"Not I. I didn't even know half the songs. I just played some chords to go with them. The credit's yours, Bertie." But Ruth was warmed by the praise, and exhilarated by the unexpected happiness she had felt while playing with them. The idea came to her that this was something she could do with her children and their friends. She watched Bertie shepherding the rest of the group into the dining room. Look at her, she thought, completely unaware of her gift, keeping everyone peacefully in hand. She must be a superb coach.

Bertie put her head around the doorway from the dining room. "Come on, everybody's waiting for you."

"Sorry," Ruth said, and she hurried along after her, feeling like a dilatory schoolgirl.

It was almost as if there had been an agenda for the day, Rita thought, with Bertie as social director: Sports in the morning, an old-fashioned sing in the afternoon, home movies in the evening. Well, not home movies but the next thing to it. She was sunk uncomfortably in a long sofa, with Pez on one side, Jan on the other, and the rest hanging over their shoulders. Family photographs were passing from hand to hand.

Until now, each one's life since college had hardly intruded on their reunion. Offhand remarks had served to sketch in details of marriages and careers that hadn't been included in their sporadic correspondence. She had been surprised to learn that Pez's husband was a bank president in Springfield, that before she had married him she had gone from clerk to treasurer of Cortemp Industries. Agnes's astute comments about politics, growing out of her involvement with agricultural committees, impressed her. Jan had been a senior editor at Hancock-Schafer before she married the head of their textbook department. Only Hope and Ruth seemed to have settled single-mindedly into marriage—ironic, she thought, because they had seemed the most independent of the group, except for herself. She had never understood or gotten along with Hope, but she had always admired Ruth as an intellectual peer, superior even, in some fields. Yet she had never been able to get close to Ruth, who seemed to wear her Europeanism like a protective coat. For that matter, she had never felt close to any of them. Even Bertie, silly old Bertie, was better at that than I, she thought.

"That's Peter Junior and Lucy with Big Peter and me behind them," Pez was saying. Rita had seen similar ones before, in Pez's annual Christmas cards. Agnes's children, too, and Bertie's daughter, a new photo every year. Her interest was stirred, though, by pictures of the others. Ruth's husband, she knew, was a lawyer, and a good one, well thought of. Their children looked more like him than her. One picture shocked her. Ruth was standing off to one side, looking like a lonely stranger. I would have left that one at home, Rita thought.

She was surprised by Jan's and Hope's photographs. Each had brought just one; more would have been superfluous. Serene parents, happy children, all smiling, not for the camera, but simply out of unmistakable joy in being together. Even the family dogs looked contented. Wholesome was the word that came to mind. Yet even as Hope leaned over Jan to point to her husband,

Rita could feel the strength of what flowed between them. It was a contradiction of everything in the pictures. How could two people with that twist manage such clearly happy marriages?

She pushed herself back into an upright position, hoping that they'd soon finish. She was beginning to suffer from a prime case of fidgets. She felt someone's hands on her shoulders as she straightened her back. It was Ruth, gently rubbing her neck, then pulling her head back to rest against her breast. She felt herself go rigid. Every nerve jumped and she was suddenly hot, as if with fever. She felt something close to panic. She couldn't recall that anyone had ever touched her in this way.

Ruth said, "Poor Rita, you must feel like Gulliver, overwhelmed by little ones. Come, everyone, let's let Rita escape."

Not wanting to, she pulled herself away from Ruth and struggled up from the couch. Everyone was looking at her and she wondered if her face was giving her away. Once on her feet she was able to gather her composure enough to deny that she had been bored. "No, it's not that. I enjoyed the pictures, honestly. Who would have thought it, fifteen years ago?" Her voice sounded artificial to her, and the bright protest false. "I am tired, though. How about a round of nightcaps and then to bed?"

"Rita," Hope said, "I'm with you. I thought I was the only one. All that family talk has left me with a giant thirst."

Rita was sure she was only imagining that Hope had somehow sensed her unease and was trying to help her overcome it. Still, if it was so, she was grateful.

Pez apologized for them all. "We got carried away, I'm afraid. Inflicting six sets of family pictures on you all at once was unfair."

"Look at it this way, though," Jan said. "It's terrific practice for developing judicial patience."

Bertie suggested they have their drinks upstairs. "I brought the makings, and if Pez and Agnes and Ruth don't mind our using their room—"

"It's all right with me," Agnes said, "if you promise we'll get to bed sometime. Fifteen years ago you had a party in my room and it went on so long I missed breakfast. Remember?"

Rita remembered that party. She had walked out on them in disgust, and it was only after a long battle with herself that she decided not to report them to the house committee.

Afterwards, just before they went to their rooms, Ruth took her aside. "You must look at us more deeply, you see. If we are sometimes childlike, that doesn't mean we are children." It was a strange thing to say, Rita thought. She tried to consider its implications, but the three stiff drinks Hope had fixed for her had muddled her mind. She took Ruth's hands in her own and studied them carefully. "Piano hands," she heard herself saying, stupidly, and she quickly let go.

The gray, wet weather still hung over them on Saturday. At breakfast Bertie said, "All I can smell is mildew. It's awful."

"Maybe your nose has mildewed," Hope suggested cheerfully. No one laughed.

Agnes turned from the window. "At least it's good for the flowers. I've never seen such zinnias and snapdragons. And the roses—they're unbelievable. Look at the arbor down past the garden. You can't see the leaves for the blossoms."

"Our resident Pollyanna," Rita commented. "Next you'll be telling us how lucky we are not to have sunburns."

"I'm for going ahead with Bertie's plan for a picnic out at Osprey Point," Jan said. "The rocks and the beach would be fun. What's the difference if we get wet from the rain or the surf?"

Pez cast her vote. "Let's do it. I'd like to look for sand dollars and sea urchins for Petie's shell collection."

"You won't find sand dollars at the Point," Rita said, "except maybe fragments. They shatter on the rocks." Pez looked disappointed and Rita wished she hadn't sounded so abrupt. More gently, she added, "But I've seen sea urchins there. All right, I'll go along."

"I'll make it four," Hope said.

Agnes and Ruth said they, too, were game. Bertie, her eyes too bright, bent down and retied her sneakers. "Off we go, then. We'll stop for bread and cold cuts and stuff on the way. Bring your knapsack, Pezzie. I bet we'll find some shells, moon shells and dogwinkles at least."

By the time they had outfitted themselves in sweaters and windbreakers, packed Bertie's big station wagon with blankets and towels, and bought food and wine for lunch, everyone's spirits had improved. The gloomy drizzle had stopped, the air was cooler, if no drier, and there was a brisk breeze. The road to Osprey Point, tamped into the spine of the promontory leading from South Headland to the ocean, seemed to take them out to sea, as if they were in a solitary vessel leaving safe harbor.

Agnes used the half-hour drive to educate Ruth, whose exposure to nature had been mostly limited to city parks, about the roadside wildflowers. Jan and Hope, squeezed together in the middle of the back seat, were quiet most of the way, with Rita and Pez talking across them, replaying yesterday's golf game and then going on to talk about Pez's husband.

"It took him six years to turn me into a golfer," Pez said. "He's a patient man, but he says bankers have to be. He waited eight years for an assistant vice presidency and another six for a vice presidency. Now, after ten more, he's president."

He must be considerably older than Pez, Jan thought. Maybe that was why she had gained so little confidence over the years. A kind of child-bride aura still clings to her. All too aware of Hope pressed against her, she made herself join the conversation. "From what I know," she said, "that's meteoric for banking. But publishing isn't much better, if Dick is any example. Getting onto the first team is hard enough; breaking out on top is really tough. These days too many companies are bringing chief executive officers in from outside." She recalled Dick's bitter disappointment at being passed over and realized that it was the first time in the weekend that she had thought wholly of him. She tried to picture what he might be doing at that moment. Then she had to brace herself to keep from toppling over as Bertie swept grandly around a curve in the road.

Hope felt Jan's hand and wrist wedged between them. "Bertie, take it easy. I'm beginning to feel like a flattened gumdrop."

"It's not much further," Bertie said. "Hang on, Hope, and don't let your sugar rub off. You need every bit of sweetness you have."

"May your mildew grow mildew," Hope replied. When they arrived at Osprey Point Beach she crawled out stiffly and made a half-hearted attempt at a few calisthenics. Bertie faced her and began counting, and almost involuntarily the rest joined in. It wasn't long before the effort collapsed in gasps of laughter and short-windedness. "I think we dropped a few years on the drive out," Ruth said. "I'm glad we came."

The wine made lunch boisterous. They scorned the picnic tables on the grass on top of the cliff and climbed down to eat on the rocks below, joined by scavenging sea gulls. Pez found the gulls frightening and made no secret of her nervousness. Rita teased her. "Look them right in the eye and face them down." Pez made a heroic effort at indifference. Ruth moved closer to her. "I don't blame you," she said. "Filthy things."

While they were eating, the wind shifted and grew stronger, until it was coming straight off the ocean in gusts, each stronger and lasting longer than the one before. Keeping pace, the surf swelled in successively broader, higher waves, booming against the rocks and hurling dense volleys of water as high as thirty feet into the air and across the outermost triangle of the Point. But the uniform gray of the sky had broken into separate dark clouds and the west was brighter.

"The weather's breaking," Hope shouted to Jan.

"Yes, but which way?"

"Right on top of us," Bertie said.

Rita scattered the last of her bread for the gulls and stood up. "All right, let's go out and find Pez some sea shells." Her words were just a little slurred, Jan thought, but perhaps it was the wind. She couldn't have had that much wine. On the other hand, Rita had never been a drinker.

Bertie exploded. "Are you out of your mind? There's wet moss and seaweed all over those rocks. We'd break our necks. And if anyone fell in, even the best swimmer among us couldn't survive in that surf."

"Oh come on," Rita said. "We don't have to go all the way out. Who's coming?" It was a dare, startlingly childish, Rita in one of her rare lapses.

Pez picked up her knapsack and after a few seconds Agnes got to her feet. The three of them started out, making their way quickly over the nearer boulders, moving more cautiously as they worked their way farther out.

Then it began to rain, not the drizzle of the previous day, but a hard, steady rainfall, dumped from the heavy clouds that were now pushing inland. As the four who had stayed behind watched, Agnes slipped. Rita and Pez reached for her quickly, pulling her up between them. She seemed to be arguing violently with them, then she turned and started back. Once again she fell, this time into a mucky pool between the rocks.

"Darn fools," Bertie said. Her face, pale and worried, was shiny with rain. "I suppose we'll have to go get them."

By then Rita was well out, peering into crevices and occasionally reaching down to pick up a shell. Pez was not far behind her. Unable any longer to watch them heedlessly inching their way closer to the Point, Jan slid down the high boulder they had been sitting on and scrambled out towards them. Hope, Bertie, and Ruth followed. In seconds they reached Agnes, who was retching violently from the salt water and scum she had swallowed.

"Ruth, help Agnes up the path to the top of the cliff."

Hope's voice was scarcely audible in the noise of the breakers and the increasing wind. She stood up and shouted to Rita and Pez, but they were down among the rocks now, still gathering shells, equally oblivious to the calls of alarm and the rapidly encroaching surf.

There was a sudden lull. The wind stopped for a long moment and the water streamed off the rocks as if sucked back by the sea. Bertie stood up and shouted. "Rita! Pez! Come back!" Her face was contorted with the effort of shouting. Rita and Pez climbed back up onto the rocks, looking in at the others, who were wildly signaling out toward the Point. Pez turned first, in time to see a breaker the size of a huge truck, driving in from the northeast. She leaped for Rita and pulled her toward her, falling backward with Rita on top, just as the breaker crashed down on top of them, flattening them on the rocks like a pair of rag dolls.

As the sea drew back it pulled them with it. Jan saw Rita, with Pez still trapped beneath her, clutching at the drenched rock surface for handholds. Then she slid helplessly down into a crevice. Pez, unable to help herself, was washed farther out, almost to the Point, where the rocks tumbled into the sea.

Bertie, in the lead now, reached Rita, leaped over the crevice where she was trapped, turned, and stretched an arm down to her. "Hurry up. Got to help Pez." Somehow she pulled Rita out and towed her, stumbling, further onto the Point. By the time she reached Pez, Hope and Jan had caught up. Sensing Bertie's intention, they locked arms and Hope snatched at Rita. As soon as Bertie got a firm grip on Pez, they all strained to move back over the rocks.

It was no use. Once again a breaker rose out of the sea and slammed down upon them. Hope and Rita momentarily lost their grip on each other as they were thrown between the rocks. But by then Agnes and Ruth had come back to help. Together, struggling inland a few yards at a time, holding on as the surf broke over them, slipping out again occasionally but stopping as someone found purchase in a crevice, they all reached the safety of the high boulders under the cliff.

They lay recovering for a long while, unmindful of the storm. Finally Bertie said, “Sweet Jesus, that was close.”

Rita made a choking sound and they all looked around at her. She had moved closer to Pez, who was only semi-conscious, and put her arm around her. Even in the heavy rain they could see her weeping. “She saved me, didn’t she? Oh God, I’m so sorry.”

No one answered, until Pez finally stirred. Still dazed, she said, “Did anyone pick up my knapsack?”

Agnes started the laughter, the others joined her, and their shock and fear began to subside. Only Rita, her face turned away, refused to smile. She stood up and looked around at them all.

“How can you be laughing? We nearly all drowned, and it was my fault.” She had begun to tremble. “My God, I’m sorry,” she said again.

“Forget it, Rita,” Hope said. “We didn’t, so that’s the end of it. Now who’s for going back and getting dried out?”

They wrapped themselves up in towels and blankets for the drive back to the inn, but even so they were cold and shivering by the time they arrived. Bertie gently pulled Rita from the car while Agnes led Pez inside. Ruth, Jan, and Hope set about unloading the car and putting it away.

“Rita looks terrible,” Jan said. “Do you think she’ll be all right?”

“After a while, I think,” Ruth said. “It may take her some time to get over the shock. I doubt that any of her vain, silly lapses ever got her into such trouble before. She acted badly, so badly that even she can’t rationalize her way out of it.”

“Badly? It wasn’t bad, just foolish. Anyone might have acted the same way.”

“Not for the same reasons. Pure ego, not Pez’s shell hunt,

made her dare everyone out onto the Point, and she knows it. A situation got out of hand and it was entirely her fault. I think Rita is sick with shame, probably for the first time in her life." Ruth smiled at them. "The rest of us know that one survives these times of remorse, but she doesn't—yet."

"I feel sorry for her," Hope said.

"Don't let her know that. Anyway, Bertie will help her. If anyone can help her, Bertie can."

Bertie ran the water as hot as she dared and filled the tub. Rita, huddled in towels, sat on a stool and stared at the wall. She didn't move when Bertie said, "Okay, in you go," and finally Bertie simply pulled her to the tub, sat her on the edge, and eased her into it. Then she knelt on the floor alongside, as a mother might to bathe a child.

"Rita, don't be a dummy. Here, hang onto the soap. Honest to God, you'd think you'd committed some horrible sin. You were just a little pig-headed that's all. Now scrub, darn it."

Gradually Rita responded to Bertie's half-sympathetic, half-disgusted hectoring. When Bertie tried to wash her back, she snatched the washcloth from her and did it herself. Bertie rambled on. "You're so stiff-necked I don't believe it. I'd give anything to have someone scrub my back. Nobody to do it for me now. Bonnie's too little, and Tom and I separated last spring. His secretary. I hate secretaries. Don't tell the others. I couldn't bear the sympathy. Got to get over the sense of failure first."

Startled out of her self-absorption, Rita said, "Bertie, that's rotten."

"Oh shut up. Yes, it's rotten. Forget it, will you? Just keep in mind that you're not the only single among us now." Bertie's bitterness left her as quickly as it had come. "Look, you've been in there long enough. My turn now. You get yourself dried and dressed—I put slacks and a sweater on your bed—while I shower. Then we'll rustle up a drink and find the others."

"Is Pez all right?"

"Of course she's all right. Just chilly and maybe bruised a little, like the rest of us. She's probably more upset over losing those sea shells than anything else."

Dinner was a quiet gathering. The light-headed relief they had given way to at Osprey Point was replaced by a sober awareness that disaster had been very close that afternoon. No one had dessert, and after coffee they drifted from the table, Ruth to the piano, Jan and Hope out into the clearing night, the rest, over Rita's protests, to the card table for a half-hearted game of bridge.

There was still enough light in the west to see Eastpoint Harbor, the long jetties running from the sea wall out into the bay, and the fishing boats moored there. Looking at them, thinking of the respect fishermen have for the sea, Jan was almost sickened by the folly of that afternoon's adventure. How stupid they had been. Not just Rita, all of them. She looked at Hope. "I feel a little queasy."

"Me, too. There wasn't time to be scared this afternoon, but I'm making up for it now."

They walked in silence for a while. Then Jan said, "Everyone was brave. It was the one good thing about it."

"Good old romantic Jan. That wasn't bravery, that was desperation."

"I'd forgotten how cynical you can be. I'm sorry, I didn't mean that."

"It's all right. Better you should think me cynical than mean-spirited, which is what I sometimes think I am. When I needle Rita, for instance."

"Mostly you've been justified."

"Not really."

They walked out to cliff's edge and looked across at the college. "Bertie wants to stop at North Tower tomorrow," Hope said. "I'm not sure I'll go along."

"Why not, for heaven's sake?"

"If you have to ask, then you'd never understand even if I tried to tell you." Hope turned, angrily. "I'm going to bed. I feel as if I'd been scrambled by a giant eggbeater."

"I'll come too."

The others had gone up by the time they got indoors. They picked up their key and slowly walked upstairs to their room. Not speaking they took turns in the bathroom and got into their beds.

As she turned off her light, Hope said, "I'm sorry I was irritable. It's the after-effects, I guess."

"That's all right. Good night."

The trouble with never being alone, Hope thought, is that you never get to weep. It might be comforting, even pleasant, to have a good, sloppy cry. She shifted from her back to her side, vaguely aware of a pattern of aches that began with her face and extended all the way to her ankles. Thinking they would do as well as sheep for counting, she began a mental list. The tender spot between her eyes was where Rita's elbow had caught her, the wrenched shoulder was where she'd gotten jammed in a crevice, the sore ribs—

Jan interrupted. Her voice was high and strained, and seemed very far away. "Hope, are you awake?"

"Yes. Every miserable inch of me."

"Come here. Please. I want you to hear my heart."

Sunday morning was clear and breezy. the sky was bright, sunlight bouncing off the village houses and the fishing boats, glittering over the whitecaps in the harbor.

Rita knocked on Jan's and Hope's door, then went across the hall to the suite the others shared. Agnes and Pez were up, Ruth still in bed but awake.

Rita was uncharacteristically apologetic. "I'm not too early, am I? Bertie said we were to get up early."

"Of course not," Pez said. "Where is Bertie?"

"Look out the window."

Bertie was standing at the edge of the cliff, just beyond the rose arbor. She was staring out at the sea, hands on hips, her windbreaker flapping around her.

"She looks like a big sea bird, about to take off," Pez said.

Ruth got out of bed to look, then turned to the others. "She's the kindest, most unselfish person I've ever known."

"Yes," Rita said. She managed a smile. "The other night Hope said I was mother superior of this group. She was wrong. It's Bertie."

Ruth broke the silent consensus. "I suppose if I got dressed we could go down and get some breakfast." She moved too suddenly and said, "Oh, my. I must have used some muscles I didn't know I had."

Rita turned away and closed her eyes. Her words came out harshly, one by one. "I'm sorry. I'm terribly ashamed."

"Bosh," Hope said from the doorway. "I want you to know, Rita, that God has finally punished me for all the times I've been bitchy to you." She was smiling, and Jan, behind her, was laughing outright.

Hope came further into the room so they could see her face. Circling both eyes and across the bridge of her nose, as symmetrical as a mask, was a dark bruise, tinged with green. "The color's smashing, don't you think?"

"Very becoming," Ruth said gravely. "What are you going to tell your husband?"

They all laughed then, even Rita. From down the corridor an angry voice shouted, "Will you people shut the hell up?"

"Oh, my," Hope said, "we're disturbing the peace. Good thing it's our last day."

At breakfast Pez said, "I wish it weren't our last day. It hasn't been long enough. Especially since I spent the first half of the time thinking it was a mistake to have come." She looked around at them all. "There's something—"

"I expect we all had our doubts," Bertie interrupted, "even Jan and Hope."

"Especially Jan and Hope," Jan said. She looked at Hope. "Right?"

"Right. The past can be unsettling."

"I didn't finish," Pez said. There wasn't a trace of the usual high color in her face. Her voice was very low, but steady. "I have to tell you. I can't let you go on thinking better of me than I deserve. I was the one who stole the money from the bookstore. That was why I was sorry I'd come. I'd been able to stop thinking about it. Almost. But then it came back. Your innocent little Pez. All these years. Rita knew. So I guess you knew everything, didn't you, Rita?"

They all looked at Rita, all but Ruth, who got up from her place, went around to Pez, and kissed her on the cheek.

Rita was more shaken than she had ever imagined she could be. She felt a desperate need to share their lovingness, and an Alice-in-Wonderland sense of being very small and looking up at them, tall strangers sitting around the table. "It wasn't that terrible. Nothing any of you might have done was that terrible. I was the worst one, thinking myself so virtuous, judging everyone. Until yesterday I was writing you off as grown-up schoolgirls, still carrying a lot of foolish loves and loyalties around with you like old notebooks you couldn't bear to part with even though they weren't important any longer."

"I don't think they are very important," Agnes said, "except to us."

"Good God," Bertie said. Her eyes were bright and angry. "Are we going to waste this whole precious morning sitting around teary-eyed and regurgitating the past?"

It was like a stinging sea breeze, Ruth thought. Trying to think of something helpful, she surprised herself by suggesting that they all go to college chapel. Why, she wondered. She could count on her fingers the number of times she had gone to chapel in their undergraduate days, and she hadn't been in a church since, except for weddings and funerals.

Hope looked relieved. She pushed her chair back, making a great clatter, and said, "Good idea. Chapel and then we'll look in at North Tower. Back to the nunnery."

Later, on their way back to the inn, Agnes walked with Pez. "Do you feel better for having told us?"

"No," Pez said. She was still very pale.

"I thought not. It's not that any of us thinks less of you. It's just that it wasn't the way to make yourself feel better about it. If it will cheer you up any, I have my own painful memory to carry around from those years, too. Not one that I could ever talk about it. I can't even talk to myself about it."

"But it wasn't the same at all," Pez said.

Agnes stopped in the middle of the path. "What do you mean?"

Pez blushed. "Getting pregnant. It wasn't the same."

"You knew I was pregnant?"

"Oh, Aggie, you were so dumb. No one can hide it. Unless she's fat as a sow to begin with, and you weren't."

Agnes could almost feel herself falling apart. She began to laugh, and unable to stop, she laughed until Pez took her by the shoulders and shook her violently. When she could control her voice again, she asked, "Did everyone know?"

"All of us in North Tower, I guess. We never talked about it, at least I don't think anyone did. I suppose we all just worried about it a lot, what you were going to do. What finally happened? No, I take that back. It's none of my business."

"I don't want to talk about it. Dear God, what a fool."

"No. It was like me stealing and not realizing that I should have just returned the money. Or like Jan and Hope, thinking it was wrong to love each other. We just didn't know how to cope with things then."

"Do we now?"

"A little better, I think. At least none of us would deny the obvious now. That's something. You know, Aggie, you really have made me feel better. Thanks."

Agnes couldn't smile. "You're welcome. I wish I could say the same."

Rita and Ruth finally gave up waiting for Bertie, who was still wandering through North Tower, and made their way slowly down to the harbor and back up to the inn.

"I don't remember that it was so stuffy and smelly up there," Rita said. "It must be that our olfactory nerves were less sensitive in those days."

"The walls have had fifteen more years to accumulate smells," Ruth said. "I'm quite sure it wasn't that bad when we lived there."

"I could have missed this part of the weekend entertainment. Except," Rita added quickly, "that it would have upset Bertie."

"It's been a remarkable time," Ruth said. "I never would have thought that the whole group would lapse so easily back into the relationship we had in college."

"How else would it have turned out? We wouldn't have behaved like seven strangers. You're not entirely right, though, about all of us falling into the old patterns. I started out the same, but along the way I stumbled badly." Again her voice was rough, betraying her difficulty in acknowledging error. "I thought about it most of the night. You know, I never developed the emotional equipment the rest of you have. That's what was wrong. I couldn't form the attachments everyone else did."

"You're already beginning to make up the lost time." Ruth paused. "You are astonishing, Rita. So analytical. To look at yourself objectively and then deliberately change yourself. Most of us can't do that."

Rita put her hand on Ruth's arm. "I'm not capable of changing. Maybe some, but not quickly and never completely. It's too late. I think my affections will always be stunted. But this weekend helped. Everyone helped, most of all you and Bertie."

"This weekend helped all of us." Ruth said, "except Bertie. I'm afraid it will end in new pain for her."

"She should come back here to live. She could find work."

"It might help," Ruth said, "but it's not just the place Bertie needs. It's us—the sisterhood, Agnes called it."

After lunch Jan said she would drive Hope to the airport in Boston, to save her the long bus trip. The goodbyes at the inn were made easier by Bertie, who assured them she would see to it that they all got together again soon. If any of them doubted it, none of them would have hurt Bertie by saying so, but Jan had sensed a not altogether reluctant pulling apart, a loosening as each turned to home.

They were out of Eastpoint and heading south on Route One when Hope said, "We left Bertie alone. Jan, let's go back. Please. Even though I may miss my plane."

It took twenty minutes and Jan was sure that Bertie would have left, but when she wheeled into the driveway at the inn there was the big station wagon, loaded with Bertie's luggage, ready to go. There was no sign of Bertie.

"She'll be out by cliff's edge," Hope said.

She was, sitting on the ground with her legs drawn up and her arms resting on her knees, looking across to the college. Hope sat down on one side, Jan on the other. Bertie was crying.

"It was a wonderful party, Bert," Hope said. "Except for the weather, and you couldn't help that."

"Next time it's got to be even better," Jan added.

"You've got a long drive ahead," Hope said. "Don't you think you should get started?"

Without looking at either of them, Bertie stood up and walked off toward her car. They could see her mopping her eyes, so they waited briefly before catching up to her.

“This is the bad part,” Bertie said. “It’s just like fifteen years ago. So hard to leave.”

“It’ll be all right in a few days,” Jan said. “You’ll see.”

“Maybe. As good as it can be. Anyway, there’s always next time.” She stopped. “But the rest of you don’t really think there’s going to be a next time, do you?”

“Yes, Bert, there will be,” Hope said firmly. “You bet there will be.”

Of Nature

Mountain Pinks

They bloom each spring in sweet abundance.

To capture their beauty, bring it close,
I bring vase and shears, reach in,
as trembling leaves brush my face
and spreading limbs embrace me.

My hand is stopped—by a butterfly.

Not mine alone, this unearned gift.
The vase stays empty, yet my need is filled—
Content to breathe, touch gently, wonder,
I leave the nectar to another.

Invasions

My neighbor's wild blue violets
    slip westward, beneath the fence
    that separates our lands.
My ferns, indifferent,
    make no effort to eject
    their uninvited guests,
for their own persistent runners
    have already tunneled eastward,
    to push up green fronds
that will reign over all:
    the parent violets,
    the trillium and lady's slippers,
and all the other occupants
    who share a nurturing earth
    that knows no fence.

Moving In

He is on the roof, taking in the view,
while from below she voices her concerns.
In rising tones, she tells him of her needs.
He descends, goes in, looks around, comes out.
Their survey now concluded, they begin,
first to clear the former owner's leavings,
then furnish and adorn their new home.
The entrance, though, is small; they must push,
turn, and heave each piece, scolding all the while.
The forked bedpiece is the greatest challenge,
but his long, tenacious, stubborn struggle
eventually succeeds. She takes over,
carries in the soft and fragrant bedding.
The enterprise consumes a day and more,
but finally they're done and satisfied.
How do we present a gift of welcome
to our industrious new neighbors—the Wrens?

Redbreasts in Charge

We don't wait for dawn
still enclosed by night,
to herald the new day.

Now's the time to rise
and sing aloud our readiness
to reclaim earth and sky.

We briefly stretch and preen
then look to feed the young,
reaming neighbors' gardens.

We stroll familiar pathways,
sometimes fly the busy roads—
to defy that other traffic.

Rain or sun it matters not;
seek shelter, then go on;
we claim no special way.

Evening comes to dim the day,
to hush the worldly noise
of those who now want silence.

We wait till all is still,
then face the growing dark—
and trumpet in the night.

Limited Access

Starting up the hill at sixty....
Wait, slow down, slow down!
There's something up ahead,
Skittering across the highway.

A bird? Walking across the road?
Sure enough, a middling-sized black bird.
Why doesn't it fly? Because...
It's leading four little ones.

They're walking, not running,
With no notion of the danger.
There they go now, into the grass,
Under the No Passing sign.

You're asking me for reasons?
To search for food and water;
To escape from danger, maybe.
Their journey, in fact, much like ours.

The Dying Elm

Here, beneath the dour winter sky,
the observer cannot know
your towering branches will not again
bear leaves—
sees only limbs drawn to the light above,
dominating your lesser comrades,
branching outward to protect
the huddled life below—
nor know your rise to grandeur,
then the cruel and crippling plague
that stripped you of your strength
and stole your promised life.

The observer cannot know—sees you
no less majestic in your final season
than in your princely youth.

Insight

Never mind being humbled
    by the vast expanse of the sea.
Simply stand at surf's edge
    and see yourself reflected
in the bubble at your feet—
    image dwindling upward,
then bursting into emptiness.

"Keepsakes"

WHEN SHE was told, Libbeth had a vague notion that she might have some control over when and where it would happen. So she designated a year from July, in the back yard of her little saltbox in York, and set about planting her garden.

I.

His shadow preceded him across the lawn and dropped over her hands as she dug around the zinnias.

"Hello, Libbeth."

She shaded her eyes as she looked up into the afternoon sun. At first she didn't know him; then he shifted and she saw his face clearly.

"Ned." She said it quietly, but she was surprised. "What in the world are you doing here?"

"One of those chance things. I had business in Ceylon and since I was in the neighborhood I thought I'd look you up." He folded himself down on the grass beside her.

She laughed. "You came upriver by the afternoon packet, no doubt. Staying at the Planters Club?"

"No, my dear, with you, if you'll have me. I'm sure your gin is better."

"You always were a bit cheeky, Rodney. But it happens Edmund is out checking monsoon damage to the tea leaves, so you can have his quarters. Here let me take your bush jacket."

"Can't. I have a hole in my crumpets-and-tea shirt."

They broke into unrestrained laughter. He said, "I've never wanted to play that game with anyone but you."

"But have you?"

"I tried once, with a girl I rebounded with. First of all I had to explain it to her. Then she never saw the fun in it. I suppose it is kind of awful."

"And childish. Your friend might have thought you were too old for such nonsense."

"Stuffy, she was. But she could ski rings around me. And did. That's how I broke my leg."

"She sounds like an unfortunate choice."

"Yes and no. I gave up skiing and saved buckets of cash; that was fortunate. But between you and her, I came away determined never to marry. So I'm still a bachelor. How's Stan?"

"He died four years ago. In a car accident."

"Oh, Libbeth, I'm sorry."

"He was a fine man." She hesitated for only a moment. "I've wondered sometimes what would have happened if I'd met you first."

"You were so damned principled. Oh well, we've only lost a little time. Why don't we get married now?"

"Ned! I haven't seen you in nearly twenty years!"

"That's a poor excuse—if you mean it to be an excuse. Why not? We can't have changed all that much."

"Well, for one thing, where would we live?" She knew she couldn't take him seriously and was astonished to find herself even asking the question. The same compelling Ned.

"Wherever you want. Here, if you like. I'm flexible."

"What about your work?"

"EDP auditor. I can find work anywhere."

"It sounds dull. I thought you were going to be a writer."

"Surprisingly, it's not. But I'm writing, too. Part-time. Mostly plays."

"Oh. Well, it's an interesting idea. Marriage, I mean."

"Why don't we have dinner and talk about it?"

She sat back and looked up at him, reflectively. "You know, you're crazy."

"You told me that when we first met, but I didn't think you held it against me."

"All right, we'll have dinner and talk about it. Do you want to take me out, or shall we eat here?" Suddenly mischievous, she said, "I have a tuna casserole I can reheat, and plenty of salad makings."

"Thanks, we'll eat out. But you can give old Rodney that gin first, if you will."

He unfolded himself and stood, then reached down and helped her up. The touching of hands and meeting of eyes stirred them both. He bent and kissed her cheek, then, gently, her lips.

"Nice?"

"Definitely."

The restaurant Libbeth suggested was small and unpretentious, but the menu was varied and the food good. They ate well, reminisced, and spoke of their lives since their last meeting. Over coffee they were silent. By the time he helped her into her coat, the mood had changed. Libbeth felt almost melancholy. He was thoughtful and remote.

"I think it would be best if I didn't stay at your place after all. The neighbors, you know."

When they reached her house again the evening air was unpleasantly cool and damp.

"Come on in for a few minutes. We can have a cordial and take the chill out."

After a few sips she said, "Do you still like a cigar once in a while? I don't mind if you smoke."

"Thanks, but not this evening. That's good liqueur. I feel a lot better."

Finally Libbeth said, "It was fun thinking about it, Ned, but it won't work."

He sighed. "I guess not. Just another poor script."

"The trouble," she said, "is the ending. It's simply too pat."

"In that case, dear girl, I think I'd best nip into my trench coat and be off. This fog is tricky in the streetlights. One can barely find one's way to Whitehall and the inspector needs every man he can muster tonight." His smile was a pale thing.

"Come back, Ned. Will you do that once in a while?" She took his hand and held it to her cheek for a moment.

"Sure. Next time we might get it to work."

II.

"Why did you name me Beth?" Her daughter had driven down to say goodbye. "People are forever saying, 'No, no, your full legal name, Miss Carlisle.' And I'm forever explaining that Beth *is* my full name. Where's my birth certificate?"

"Your father chose Beth. Be glad you're not another Libbeth, which was what he first wanted. Nobody can spell Libbeth. And you've lost at least five copies of your birth certificate in five years; there must be one there someplace." She studied the sunburned face and added, "Why is it, honey, that you never get an even tan?"

"I forget to rotate. I haven't got time for those niceties, Ma." There was just a hint of irritation.

"I'm not suggesting that you rotate. It just occurred to me that the law of averages says you should have had at least one even tan in twenty-three years." She laughed, to cover a quick memory of those auburn curls bent over the same table twenty years ago. Her most independent, but most loving child.

"Have they told you yet how long this assignment will be?"

"No less than a year. Not worth the trouble to send me for any shorter time." Beth looked up from the scattered sheets of applications, references, and transcripts. "I'll miss you, Ma. But I'll write."

"Yes. Me too." Libbeth turned away, made a great to-do of looking at the lamb roast in the oven, and began carrying silverware into the dining room.

"Gosh, we're being kind of fancy, aren't we? Who all's coming?"

"Just Fran and Uncle Bob. Oh, and an old friend from my flaming youth. He came through town a month or so ago and he's coming back this way again. Hope you don't mind. But you'll like him, I promise."

Beth studied her mother keenly. "Are you blushing? Oh boy, an old love. Maybe you'll be married the next time I see you."

"And maybe I won't. Why don't you concentrate on your own business and get that table cleared so I can fix the salad? Better still, you can fix the salad. Here." She tossed a tomato at her daughter, then remembering the vital papers, instantly wished she hadn't. But Beth caught it, and only a drop of tomato squirted out. She wiped it off her passport.

"Ha! The same old eagle eye and quick reflex. Remember the year you coached the softball team?"

"I certainly do. Won four, lost eight, tied three. We had no pitching. Now clear off and get busy with the salad."

The evening was a huge success. At Uncle Bob's suggestion, they played charades after dinner. Everyone was good at the game, and it was perfect for making Ned feel wholly comfortable, although Libbeth had had no misgivings on that score. His absurd greeting had set them all to laughing right away. "The mail steamer to Macao. Does it stop here?"

Sharp, quick Fran, who'd known of Ned for years although they'd never met, fielded that one. "Sorry, sailor, it sank two years ago. Now we get only junk mail."

Even Ned was awed at that, and he studied Fran respectfully for a full half hour before further conversation with her.

It was two o'clock when the party ended, and almost three when Libbeth and Beth finished cleaning up.

"Night, Ma. I have to leave at eight-thirty. Sure you want to get up with me?"

"Now, yes. Tomorrow, no. But I will."

She was rewarded in the morning with a cup of coffee delivered while she dressed hastily. Beth burst out laughing when she got downstairs. "Ma, it's bad enough for you to be wearing my old barn jacket, but you've got it buttoned crooked." She rebuttoned it, gave Libbeth a quick kiss, and got in her car. Then she got out, ran back, and gave her a fierce hug. "It won't be long." The old car careened off like a startled horse.

III.

Uncle Bob waited a full week before he came around. She wished him there at least a dozen times in the interval, but thought each time that she was better off coping alone. When he did come, he had fishing gear for them both and a new windbreaker for her.

"You can't be running around on my boat in that disreputable farmer's coat," he said.

Her mother had died when she was two, and Uncle Bob had helped her father raise her. He'd been everything Dad wasn't. Or, more fairly, Dad had been everything Uncle Bob wasn't. Dad had worked hard around the house, gone to the plant every day, and helped her with her homework. Uncle Bob had worked as little as possible, played the horses, and taken her sailing. It had been a happy childhood, and if she missed having a mother, she had been blessedly unaware of it.

The sun was hot, but she was grateful for the windbreaker before they even cast off. The breeze was onshore, and brisk. "You take the jib," he ordered, unnecessarily because she'd been assigned to the jib for years, since the first time she'd been old enough to crew for him. They beat out slowly and it was almost two hours before they dropped anchor at their favorite fishing spot.

"Beef or salami?"

"How's the salami?"

"Spicy."

"One of each."

It was as predictable as the course of the sun. She'd once brought sweet pickles instead of dills and he'd reproached her for years. The time she forgot the beer he vowed never to trust her again, and from then on he was the one who kept the locker stocked.

"How long will Beth be gone?"

"At least a year, she thinks."

"Goddamn. That's too long. These kids have no sense of responsibility, no family loyalty. First chance and they're off."

Libbeth couldn't believe it. "You're a fine one to talk. Who was it ran away at seventeen and joined the Merchant Marine? And never came home for eight years? And left a poor, broken-hearted mother?"

"That's a bit thick, Libby." He looked at her defiantly. "Besides, that was different. It made an honest man of me instead of a bum. Well, it made me an honest bum, at least."

"Beth has a first-rate job and this is a marvelous opportunity and you know it." She said it mildly, because she wouldn't have changed him for all the world.

They caught no fish that day and Uncle Bob grumbled all the way back to York because the wind had changed and it took them as long to get home as it had to get out.

"Why don't you take me to the lobster pound for supper?" she asked.

"It's a poor man you'll be making of me, Niece. But the idea has merit. Tell you what—you stand for the drinks and I'll treat to the lobster."

This, too, was traditional. "Not on your life, you old Scrooge. You owe it to your crew."

They walked home, singing "Galway Bay" in an off-and-on harmony that had been the best they could manage for all their years together. But they sang softly, because the town constable had once had to come to the house and deliver a neighbor's complaint. That was the first time Libbeth had ever had a drink. The embarrassment it had caused Dad was still a painful memory to them both. Uncle Bob had hung his head and nearly wept, saying, "Now Willie, now Willie," quite ineffectually. And Libbeth had worried for a week, fearful that she'd never be allowed to go sailing with Uncle Bob again. But Dad had never said a word to her about it. She didn't think he'd had to say anything to Uncle Bob, either.

IV.

Libbeth couldn't remember when Fran hadn't been near, from their childhood, when they'd squabbled bitterly over toys and in rough neighborhood games, through an intense adolescent friendship, to a comfortable next-door companionship that had begun when she and Stan came home from their wedding trip.

When Stan died, Fran met her at home. They'd had coffee. After a long silence, Fran had said, simply, "It's a rotten life," and left Libbeth with the children gathered soberly around her.

Fran was in and out as usual after Beth left, and they made their unhurried, haphazard rounds of markets, meetings, and occasional outings. Early in October they drove north, mostly on back roads. The foliage was beginning to change and there was a nice brilliance in the long views of the bright maples and birches, especially against the evergreens.

"But I like oaks best, for some reason," Fran said. "They're so solid, and they just change to a nice comfortable brown. No show, no vanity."

Libbeth pondered on that for a moment. "Maybe," she said finally, "but the only thing that ever impressed me about oaks was acorns. They were fun to gather up. Still are, for that matter."

"Let's stop for a walk," Fran said, "and maybe something hot to drink."

Cold as the days were becoming, there were still lots of strollers on the beach, and most exchanged nods or smiled gravely and politely as they passed. Unleashed now that the restrictions of summer were not in force, dogs ran joyously in and out of the surf. Occasionally a hardy swimmer went galloping across the beach into the breakers. Libbeth was almost tempted. This time of year the water could be warmer than the air, and ocean-swimming was not nearly as masochistic as it appeared to the uninitiated.

On the way back they stopped for tea at a small cafeteria. The causeway along the beach was almost deserted by then. As they gazed out, a young girl rode past on a bicycle, no-handed, playing a flute as she pedaled. "Oh, look, Fran." Libbeth felt compelled to hurry out and look after her. What a lovely thing to see, she thought; and she knew the picture would stay in her mind like a stopped movie frame. It made her think of Beth.

"Don't you wish you knew what she's thinking about, where she's going, what her family and home are like?"

"Nope," Fran replied. "I'm sure it's all very prosaic. She's thinking about some frizzy-haired beau, she's on her way home from a music lesson and forgetting to stop for the milk she's supposed to pick up, and she'll be getting a terrific tongue-lashing from her slatternly mother in about five more minutes."

"You're the most unpoetic person I ever knew," Libbeth said amiably.

It was late when they got home. Libbeth suggested supper together at her house. "I have some leftover casserole; be a pal and help me finish it."

"I have leftover casserole of my own, but I'll make the sacrifice. Maybe yours is better. But you'll have to give me a drink first."

It wasn't the unaccustomed drink, they later told each other. Libbeth opened the upper cupboard for plates, and brushed a potholder onto the floor. When she came up from retrieving it, she struck her head sharply on the cupboard door. The pain was immediate and overwhelming, and she barely made it to a chair. Fran was beside her in seconds. "Move your hand; let me see. My God, what a crack. Here, you broke the skin but it isn't bleeding much. Hold this wet cloth against it while I call the doctor."

He was there in less than ten minutes. After a careful examination he said, "Wouldn't be surprised if you gave yourself a mild concussion. Not much we can do for you now but watch for symptoms. Can you stay with her, Fran? I'll check back in the morning. No aspirin or anything."

By the time he left, Libbeth felt fine except for some soreness around the rising bump on her head. She was quite hungry, and they went ahead with supper. Fran hovered over her with uncharacteristic solicitude, which Libbeth found strangely annoying. "Oh stop fussing." She was immediately ashamed of herself. By the time the dishes were done, she was more than grateful for Fran's presence, and she meekly allowed herself to be put to bed.

"You don't have to stay with me. I'll phone if I need you."

"Sorry, you've got yourself an overnight guest whether you like it or not. Now go to sleep." Unexpectedly, Fran bent and kissed her; then she turned off all but one low light by a chair across the room and sat down. Libbeth smiled at her and closed her eyes.

She woke up a few times during the night, each time turning to see if Fran was still there. Each time she found her awake and reading, and each time Fran looked over at her questioningly.

"Okay?"

"Yes."

"Go back to sleep."

By morning she felt fine, although she had a grand lump. Fran looked rumpled and anxious, but after the doctor's early visit and cheerful pronouncement that the patient would be all right, she reverted to her normal brusque manner.

"Okay, let's have some breakfast and then I'm going home to change."

But before she went, over a second cup of coffee, Fran asked, "Libbeth, you're so dreamy lately. Is anything wrong?"

"No, not really. It's just been a strange summer. I feel as if I've been rummaging around in the attic and turning up old treasures. I keep seeing everything—people, mostly—in a different way. Change of life coming on, maybe."

"Are you well?" It was more of a plea than a question, and Libbeth didn't answer it. She had known Fran would guess. She looked steadily into those worried eyes. Finally she shook her head.

The anguish of the next moments was so deep that Libbeth thought they both might die right then and there. Fran came and knelt beside her. She put her head in Libbeth's lap and her arms around her waist. There wasn't a sound, but when she looked up her face was wet with tears. In the softest way imaginable she said, "You can't know how I've loved you."

"Yes. Yes, I do. Me too. Always."

That day began one of the most blissful times of Libbeth's life. She found childlike happiness in the most trivial things. Inhibitions fell away from her and she took unashamed pleasure in sensual delights. Always before she'd been undemonstrative and reserved. Now she used all her senses to the fullest. Most of all, she touched everything and everyone.

The euphoria wasn't unbroken, of course. But even in moments of depression, even when she had pain, she fell back on physical comfort. Fran was there most often, and when such moments came they clung to each other. Libbeth often thought, after shaking off these sudden, passing hours of fear, we must seem to God like a couple of scared baby monkeys.

And Ned, dear Ned. He came often now, and finally she welcomed him to her bed without a thought for the proprieties that has always restrained her before. He, like Fran, had known without being told.

Uncle Bob endured her new behavior as if she had in fact lapsed back to childhood. He suffered hugs and kisses. On their last trips on the *Libbob IV* he handed her aboard gallantly, and let her take the tiller once in a while, although his misgivings about this were plain to see. He even stopped his gruff complaining, until he realized that she missed the needling, and the chance to tease him back.

She wrote to Beth: "Don't ever regret having been away. You'd have been too sweet to tolerate, and I'd probably have spent all my time weeping—or fuming at you. Just remember that last visit home. I love you. —Ma." She folded the note and asked Fran to give it to Beth afterwards.

She was wrong about the time and place. Still, it wasn't bad. There was a fragrant wood fire going. Through her window she could see good clean snow and just a bit of the harbor beyond. Fran came and went, brisk and dry-eyed. Uncle Bob brought violets, with a genuine smell of the earth, he wouldn't say from where, and a big bottle of her favorite, Grand Marnier. The three of them and Ned, too, when he was there, had a nightcap together every evening almost until the end.

At the last she was confused, and she said, "I'll take these few things with me. But look after the others, will you, Fran? And mind those attic stairs."

Commentary

Offspring

Who lay with Necessity to parent Invention?

The tiller of earth, seeking food for each day;
The diligent hunter, in search of more prey;
The builder of shelters, from woodland trees;
The first questing sailor, to venture the seas;
The territorial warrior, to slaughter his foes;
The wandering trader, to travel more roads;
The maker of garments, for sweaters and hoods;
The designer of finance, for service and goods.

All these, and more, sired Invention,
who then, in turn, with good intention,
produced an heir designed to please us—
that undisciplined child, whose name is Leisure.

Weaponry

It began with the caveman's sharpened stone
    and possibly it will end soon,
with an instrument more finely honed,
    in an obliterating firestorm.

Generations passed the skills,
    shaping, tempering, mixing, testing
tools to help the hunter kill
    for food, revenge, or territory.

Absent from this ingenuity
    any trace of human wisdom—
and growing strife brought opportunity:
    arming enemies became a business.

No longer does it cause concern
    that with destruction of a foe
innocents are lost—blown up, burned—
    "collateral damage," we are told.

Those who govern warn of danger,
    attack before they seek a reason
why the enemy's charged with hatred,
    and never ask if there's just cause.

Somewhere there's a laboratory,
    a cave lit bright through day and night,
where thickly-shielded scientists
    pursue the Weapon Ultimate.

It began with the caveman's sharpened stone,
    and possibly it will end soon,
with an instrument more finely honed,
    in an obliterating firestorm.

Saints Unlimited

Midwife in a lab coat,
    isolating cells,
    testing each for merit,
    discarding the unworthy,
delivering perfection.

Newborn without defect—
    pure in thought,
    in work, in deed,
    unadulterated virtue
to go forth in the world.

A few more generations
    of careful segregation—
    to suffocate the bad,
    perpetuate the good—
then virtue will prevail.

What then will be the purpose
    of our earthly days,
    whom then shall we guide
    in paths of righteousness
in that perfect world?

Should midwife reconsider,
    flick into the mix
    one gene of mischief,
    enlivening the future?
Or is that how it all began?

Environmental Concern

Some time ago, the statisticians
    met with the biologists,
joining in a consultation
    with the climatologists.

"You need numbers from the past,"
    said the statisticians,
"of species that have dwindled fast
    to show the politicians."

"The gold-backed worm, the phylace tree,
    the northern red-eyed volubird,"
biologists replied, "just three
    of many, as you have heard."

"That bird's decline is certain proof,"
    said the climatologists,
"of melting at the Arctic roof."
    "Agreed," said the biologists.

They pointed at the map to show
    the global diminution
of habitats and creatures both,
    lost to humankind's pollution.

The statisticians then designed
    a comprehensive survey,
and were not surprised to find
    most respondents in dismay.

Even then, the politicians,
    in discussion that went on for days,
could not agree on legislation
    that would lower heat and haze.

Statisticians and biologists
    met again and this time also—
urged by climatologists—
    invited the philosophers.

Observing, as they had for years,
    resolve lost to timidity,
the philosophers addressed their peers,
    "It's selfishness, friends, not stupidity.

The masses will not yield their comforts
    to save a few endangered birds.
Endure cold winters and hot summers
    walk more, buy less, conserve? Absurd!"

The talk went on, with no conclusion,
    the pros and cons continuing.
The hours passed with no solution
    for winning popular opinion.

As it grew late, the guard called in,
    "I'm leaving. Please turn off the lights.
Last time I left you people talking,
    you went out, and they were on all night."

Another Opinion

For this pill in my hand,
prescribed to calm my heart,
one thousand eight hundred and
seventy laboratory rats
gave their lives.

Put another way,
one thousand eight hundred and seventy luckless rats
were sentenced to die
in the cause of human comfort.

A dissenting alien voice inquires:
Living heart to living heart,
sacrifice against survival,
which of these two mammals
has done your planet greater harm?

A Walk in History

Wanting to leave his imprint,
Be remembered for what he did,
He stopped to look at his footprints
Too often.

Lament

I don't regret the absence
    of a faith I never had.
I understand the endings
    brought by circumstance or death.

I grieve, though, at a crueler loss:
    Trust, who walked with me each day,
gentling reality, soothing its stings,
    finally has stepped away.

The parting came slowly. First
    Skepticism edged in—polite,
deferring often to stubborn Trust.
    They walked together cautiously.

But then came Cynicism—
    rude, unyielding—scoffing
that Trust should see no evil, that
    Skepticism made allowances.

Now I am alone with Cynicism,
    the others driven out.
My soul's confined and out of touch
    with innocence and truth.

Paths to Righteousness

Where is that gentle Jew
who counseled love and said, "Judge not,"
who disciplined our childhood,
yet understood a doubting heart?

Did that assured teacher
despair, at last, as his teachings
were stripped of tolerance,
denying other paths to faith?

Wisdom lost to passion,
forbearance to suspicion—
souls wander off, then turn back,
Looking for that gentle Jew.

"A Convenient Place to Wait"

SHE SITS in the green leather chair in the afternoon and watches the street. She doesn't see anyone she knows; her people come in the evening.

Her door is open. She dislikes the clatter in the hall and passing visitors looking in, but the closed room is intolerable. A young couple goes by and the man's voice comes back, "There's a handsome old girl. Wonder what she's doing here." She is delighted and turns from the window to watch for their return, hoping they will look in and say hello. But she dozes off and when she wakes up visiting hours are over.

The sun is warm even in its last hour. It seems to engulf her and for one dizzy moment she feels as if the chair has been set adrift, floating in the dusty afternoon light. Then her eyes rest on the cluttered table and she rouses herself. Methodically, she sets about tidying up.

"Hi, Gram," and that cool, quick young kiss and there is her granddaughter—too thin, too restless, but sweetly attentive and full of tales that bubble up and around her till they seem to fill the room. This child is her favorite. She loves them all, but this one is never too respectful, never uneasy or awkward with her.

"I've got a surprise for you, Gram." She makes a great show of peering up and down the hall, then shuts the door partway. Out of a huge, shapeless leather bag, after much rummaging, comes a very large chocolate bar.

"I have it all figured out. You can hide it in your knitting bag." This conspiratorial game is too entertaining to explain to Annie that she is allowed to eat anything she wants, so after breaking off a few pieces she gravely slips the candy under a magazine.

They sit companionably, munching the chocolate. "It's delicious, Annie. Where did you ever find one so large?"

"At the supermarket. Two for the price of one, but I got just one. You should see the new east end market. It's fabulous. You could put two ordinary stores in it. Tommy's going to work there during school vacations."

"Who's Tommy?"

"A boy at school. He's in my chemistry class. I thought I told you about him."

"You probably did and I forgot. My mind gets a little fuzzy at times."

"That's okay, Gram. Anyhow I guess I talk so much it's no wonder you can't keep track."

She smiles at this unselfconscious tact, then asks about the new east end development. Annie's superlatives proceed at a gallop, and only occasionally does she allow herself to interpose her own recollections of the days when the east end was meadow and woods.

They talk and laugh until at last Anne says, "Off to the library for me. Got to study for an exam tomorrow." She leaves, then pops her head back around the door. "Quick, the knitting bag. Here comes Florence Nightingale."

Alone, she puts her head back and listens inwardly to her heart quieting. She waits for the nurse to come. No matter how tired she gets she leaves her lights on and sits up until someone comes to tell her she must go to bed. "In a while," she will say, and waits until they must come again. This small defiance every night gives her satisfaction.

The chair gives softly as she leans back, and the leather is cool where she moves her arm. There is an uncommon bustle today; the man down the hall says the owner is coming. She watches for him and when the big car pulls to the curb she looks to see who has come with him. He is alone today, a heavy man with a round red face and a collar so tight and starched that she swallows uncomfortably herself.

He always stops at every room and asks how things are going. Some are quick to complain but she never does. He is transparently more concerned with schedules and linens and plumbing than for her, and she barely manages a cold nod in answer to his hearty "How've you been." Little Mrs. Abercrombie, so shrunken and dried up she must certainly just vanish someday, thinks the owner is responsible for her being here and rails at him with marvelous vigor. One day she throws a glass at him and while it misses by some distance there is quite an uproar over it. Thereafter Mrs. Abercrombie is treated with respect by the nurses and with admiration by fellow patients.

Days without visitors fade one into the next. She has a calendar but frequently loses track of the date. Sundays and Fridays, always the two most different days in the week, are all the same now. She tries various ways of passing the long mornings but the knitting stays unfinished and the book half read. She is frightened one evening to realize the strange, quiet figure reflected in the window is herself and often even the hands resting on the arms of the chair seem unfamiliar. She longs to be home and about her daily chores.

Her youngest son comes to see her. He always makes her laugh. He is in fact quite a silly boy and always has been. She remembers his ridiculous boyhood pranks, always ending in family laughter except that once, when his father strapped him for putting the goldfish in the toilet. She had shared George's concern at the boy's thoughtlessness but felt he was excessive in the strapping. "Callous is a harsh word for a nine-year-old boy, George," she had said, but he had sternly insisted that the boy must learn respect for all living things. Later, with the remorseful Willy tucked in bed, they had giggled uncontrollably at the recollection of the poor goldfish.

They chat for a while, then he brings out the checkers and board. He brought them originally, she suspects, with a notion that this would be good therapy for her and at first he slyly threw the games her way. Then he started to play in earnest; now their games are long and brooding and tightly played. Some evenings he quietly puts the board away in the middle of a game, and she dimly realizes that she is not playing well, that her mind is not clear and her fingers unresponsive.

Tonight she looks forward to the game, but he is preoccupied.

"Ma, we've had another offer for the house." He has left himself open to a double jump and she jumps him, triumphantly.

"No. I'm not ready to sell." The house has been in George's family for generations. George's mother and father had died there and she and George, in the midst of raising their own family had brought her mother there and nursed her in her last years. She wants to ask her sons why one of them wouldn't move in with her but she puts it off, hoping that one of them will offer first.

"Even when you're well you won't be able to keep up the place. We could find you an apartment." He doesn't look at her and there's an odd strain in his voice. he moves, missing a jump, and she calls his attention to it.

"I don't want to live in an apartment. I don't want to stay here, either."

"I know you don't want to stay here, but it's a convenient place to wait," again the strained voice, "till we can get you settled."

He stands up and goes to the window behind her chair. "The truth of it is that we're having trouble paying the bills here. I'm afraid we have to sell the house."

She has known it would come to this. They argue, quietly and without anger, until she consents to think about it.

"Poor Willy. How do you always manage to get these unhappy assignments? Do you and your brothers draw straws or have they persuaded you that you're the only one I'll listen to?"

He has the grace to flush but then he laughs. "Sometimes you're too shrewd, Ma. We got together and talked about it and they said, 'Bill, you always had a special way with her.'" He mimics her oldest son perfectly.

He sits down at the board again, but a nurse comes in and reminds him that visiting hours are over, and he leaves. She sits staring at the unfinished game. They don't seem to be her children anymore. Before her illness they had been in and out of the big house every day, and even with their own growing-up children they had still seemed to be her boys. The house was alive with their coming and going, and she had at times felt like the matriarch of a growing tribe. Now they're strangers who visit, dutifully, bringing magazines and flowers. Self-pity seizes her and instinctively, though no one is there, she lowers her head to hide her filling eyes.

She visits the room at the other end of the hall every day. She sits there at the bedside and holds Katherine's hand. She had been overjoyed when the boys told her Kate O'Shea was coming to the home and had waited eagerly for her arrival. But they had wheeled in this pale, wispy-haired, murmuring figure and she had been too shocked to speak. Kate hasn't recognized her yet. She lies in bed with the protecting sides up, eyes open but not looking at anything, her hands and feet moving endlessly in small twitching motions.

She thinks of their schooldays, those tender years when they had been half children, half young women. They had been inseparable. Now she recalls those times as if looking into a lighted picture viewer. Bicycling and swimming and picnicking in the summer; school and skating and to the ice cream parlor for hot chocolate in the winter. Laughter and tears and confidences—she had loved Kate almost too much. Then they had met George and Will and it had all changed, but they remained close.

She has spells herself, days when she doesn't get up at all. She never remembers what happens then, but sometimes in the midst of clear consciousness she has moments when the threads seem to come loose and memories and impressions escape and become tangled. She fights to clear her head and as she recovers there is one fleeting moment, like a recollected dream, when she knows this is what happens during the spells.

She gets out of the chair and goes to wash for supper. She is proud that she can take care of herself most of the time. But every step is too slow, much too slow. She is two parts and the part that fails to work, that refuses to obey, baffles her. She stumbles and her eyes grow dark with confusion and dismay.

The doctor comes again. Though he is kind and friendly she dislikes him. She tells him she feels fine and he smiles and taps and thumps and manipulates and listens. Finally he goes, after telling her she is much improved. She is annoyed that he hasn't spoken of letting her go home.

The chair has smooth hardwood knobs at the ends of the arms and she exercises her hands by gripping them. Grip, relax, grip, relax. She is doing this when the nurse comes in with a stranger. He is tall, and he brings crisp, cold outdoor air into the room. His coat smells of tobacco and a trace of camphor.

The nurse is saying something, but she cannot quite understand. "George?" she says. "Tell Will and Kate I'll be ready right away."

"I'm not George," he says. "I'm the one who found you, don't you remember? Just stopped in to see how you're coming along."

She does remember him, and the day she fell. She had lain at the edge of the sidewalk for a long time, then he came along, then there was the ambulance and the hospital and the worried faces. "Yes, I know you, I know you," but she can't find any other words so she says it again and again. The nurse takes the man out into the hall, then comes back and closes the door. She helps her move from the chair to the bed and puts the sides of the bed up. This nurse is a large, ugly woman, but she is gentle.

She wakes up in the morning when the sun crosses her bed and reaches for the glass on the table to rinse her mouth. From her pillow she can look down into the yard and watch the dogs below. There is a mother and two pups tumbling around her. Today she asks if the puppies can be brought to her room and an attendant brings one and sets him on the bed. She reaches to touch him and the puppy nips her hand. She laughs and ruffles his head. Then, before she or the attendant can move him, he squats and wets the bed. This amuses her even more, but they are caught. The nurse is not angry, but she is very firm about removing the dog, and out in the hall she speaks sternly to the attendant.

For a moment she is passive and remorseful, then comes familiar rebellion. She calls the nurse back. "Help me out of bed." The grim sides are down, she pushes herself up. "Open the window a little." The nurse says, "Now, now, you know I can't do that. I'll get your breakfast."

As soon as the door closes she goes to the window and tries to open it. It won't give, and she almost weeps with the frustration.

She asks every day to have the window open but they never permit it. She thinks that she will never smell clean fresh air again and this turns her mind to dying. Sometimes she thinks she would welcome it, but more often she determines to go home and wait there. She can see the large, rambling porch, the immense old trees, and her beloved garden beds, and she pictures herself sitting in the sunny yard.

Her sister and brother come from the city to see her. Abby and Ted are the successes, the professional people of the family. Being the oldest, and having helped them, she doesn't share the family's awe of them, but she feels diffident with them, especially now, in this place.

They stay for a long while, talking first about their work and the people they know, then falling into reminiscences. She wishes she had fresh new experiences and people and places to share with them, but even when she tries to tell them, in her dry humorous way, of the pleasant or amusing things that happen sometimes in the home, it comes out sounding querulous, or at best dull.

So she endures the reminiscing and even occasionally enjoys the familiar recitations of old days, the family parties and weddings, the childhood escapades, the funny sad stories of relatives long since gone.

She notices that the chair has developed a sag on one side and she asks the nurse if it might be repaired. She has retied springs herself and suggests that if an attendant could be sent up she would show him how to fix the chair. Instead they take the chair away and bring her a new one.

This one is a rocking chair, not an old-fashioned rocker but a great overstuffed thing that envelops her and makes her feel quite small and helpless. Outraged, she goes to see Kate.

She closes the door before she goes to the bed. She bends over and looks hard into Kate's eyes. "I'd like to go for a walk, Kate. Come with me." There is a small flicker in the blank eyes and she takes one frail hand. "Let's go. It's a lovely day, not too cold." Deep in that dark stare there is recognition and for one brief second the hand tightens on hers. Then everything goes blank again. She sighs and presses the hand to her cheek.

Somehow she manages the stairs without falling and somehow she gets to the lower hall without being seen. She has no coat, but there are several on the rack by the door and she takes the warmest-looking one.

She has a narrow escape as she starts down the steps. Someone is coming, but luckily it is a stranger. They nod at each other. She wishes she could go faster but she is imprisoned in this slow walk.

It is a lovely tree-lined road and reminds her of the street where she grew up. George walked with her often before they were married. How they would talk, of life and people and school and books. He was shy to take her hand and she would take hold of his, laughing to feel him grow stiff and awkward. She imagines that George is walking with her now.

They find her an hour later, over a mile away. Her eyes are bright and there is a small smile on her face. She does not protest when they take her to the car and she says nothing when they chide her. She is pleasantly tired and cannot pretend to be sorry, even when they tell her how worried they were.

When they return there are her sons and her granddaughter. They seem to be at odds, and Annie looks flushed and angry. But with her arrival they crowd around and help her out of the coat. Whatever got into you, what a scare you gave us, how are you feeling, you'd better get some rest now. This chorus of solicitude irks her faintly.

"Tomorrow," she says, "I'm going home." She waits for the protests but there are none, and she decides to save her arguments until they are needed.

Her youngest son helps her to her room. As they start up the stairs she hears Annie saying, heatedly, "But Dad, why couldn't we—" and the rest of the question is muted. She half turns back to them, but Willy urges her along gently.

To her surprise the green chair is back in its accustomed place and he settles her in it. "I like a walk," she says and he smiles. She remembers to apologize for borrowing the coat and then, well satisfied, she closes her eyes.

Memories

Heaven Knows

Scuffed paint, faded curtains,
bedpost dents in the floor,
the nest of our childhood
comforts us once more,
easing the return
to say goodbye, to touch
the cold, stilled fingers
that gently shaped so much
of what we have become—
counseling, comforting
leading the way.
Useless, now, to wonder
whether their quiet spirits rest
content with their labors.
They never said. We never asked.

To Revisit the Past

No place is as we left it,
No time as we remember.
No face remains the same.
Wistful memory skews recall.

But say we did return,
Live once more the time that made us,
See those faces once again,
Would memory correspond to truth?

The shabbiness in house and garden,
The many long and tedious days,
Loved ones who then turned away—
Realities truth would demand.

Push truth aside, let memory's glow
Recreate that place of beauty,
Fill those days with adventure,
Return to us the loves we knew.

Lost and Found

I misplaced my heart—
or most of it—
somewhere in the past.

Looking for it lately,
I could not recall
where I might have left it.

Could I have dropped it,
not noticing,
when with my gentle friend?

Or did I, in anger,
throw it away,
that time I was refused?

Then you returned
from that distant time
and held out your hand:

"I found this when you left.
I've saved it—not knowing
if you wanted me to keep it?"

Another Affair

Love drifts away,
its absence scarcely noticed,
yielding to sturdier comforts:

The flowers of the garden
tossing colors at the sky,
shadowed momentarily
by a passing butterfly.

Wind-driven clouds,
indifferent to the sun
concealing evening showers
till the gardening's done.

Chipmunks, squirrels, birds
overseeing—as if they know
they, too, will reap the harvest
if they let the garden grow.

Agreeable companions,
accepting, undemanding,
but with cautious eyes intent
escape routes close at hand.

The late-day calm descends
quietly upon us all;
a peace surpassing love
erases its demanding call.

Love drifts away,
its absence never noticed.

Of Our Time

Wisdom

Oh dear and learned knight of Academe:
You seek companions for your intellect,
With whom to joust and spear some worthy theme—
An ancient scroll or tome, a scholar's text.
But those who share that noble realm are few.
'Tis not the ken of those who till the earth,
Work daily with machines, at desks, in schools,
In kitchens, or in scientific search.
Their learning's mostly from necessity;
Their wisdom, gathered as they count the years,
No less profound: Kindness, truth, and charity
For friend and adversary, without fear.
Set aside that book. Though you know so much,
It is, as with the rest of us, not enough.

Commencement Address

Not always so gracious,
nature gives us sunshine
and a gentle breeze;
while in the park beyond
sparrows align themselves
to watch from the trees.

Uncertainty and doubt
yield to confidence and hope
on this brightening day,
and new roads open—
paths among the clouds—
leading to wisdom and grace.

Among you is there one
to walk among earth's people—
every homeland, every race—
convince all that compassion,
not bloody battles and destruction,
is the only avenue to peace?

Those who went before you,
sacrificed, and failed,
attest that it cannot be done—
as well to ask the sparrow
to yield its nest, give up its seed,
relinquish rights to the warming sun.

Is there one among you,
or more, to come forward,
reach out, pull faiths together?
Or shall we, as the sparrow,
accept the present as our destiny,
and stay watchful among the trees?

Counseling

Setting household tasks aside,
she joined the weekly group of friends
seeking solace for their troubled souls.

First the analyst explained
their suffering, the likely cause
of their despair and misery.

Next came the therapeutic drills,
exercising mind and body,
to alleviate their cares.

She wondered:
Why would they not instead
send us home to do the laundry,
hang the sheets, iron the shirts,
and wash away self-pity?

Cleaning Up

The guests are gone, the music ended—
    but the gossip and the bawdy jokes,
    the retelling of the latest scandals,
    echo in her weary thoughts.

He offers to help, gathering dishes,
    scrubbing bowls and rinsing pots,
    chuckling at the recollection
    of political jabs and innuendos.

She watches as he polishes:
    He frowns at streaks and smudges,
    seeking gleaming spotlessness
    on every tray and pan.

With half a smile, she reminds him:
    "You waste your time on the outside, my dear,
    it's the inside of the pot
    that must be kept clean."

Staying Informed

Bring the news to my table:

The gritty-cheeked youth arrested
for a crime too heinous to tell—
except by insinuation.

The newly divorced cinema star,
abulge in fashion's minimum—
"but we'll always be friends."

Third from the top, gray and weary,
reporters, with the latest body count—
soldiers first, then the others.

And now the Senator—
with bandages for economic wounds,
to assure recovery.

Then the commentator,
impressively credentialed,
to analyze and foretell.

Last, the requisite note of cheer—
spunky child runs to rescue
horses from a burning barn.

I'll be back later, for more.

Going Home

Dry rocks and dust
slow the weary driver.
Drought has consumed
the shining waters.

She stops to let a crow
pluck at a fawn's remains.
At the edge of the woods
the doe stands motionless.

"Road kill," they call it here—
back there, "collateral damage."
She sees again the father
gather the child in his arms.
His tears still sting her eyes,
as now the mute grief of the doe
tightens her hand on the wheel.

Now, as then, she whispers,
"I didn't do it,"
but knows, as then, that she
is among the many
who share the guilt.

Requiescat

The ambling herds are gone.
These placid few remaining
come to the fence,
dark eyes engaging
the passerby.

The graying barn leans back,
slates weeping from its roof,
cool and dark inside,
aromas in the stalls
still lingering.

The valley floor is hushed,
the gentle lowing stilled—
meadows untrodden,
grasses growing tall—
a life work ended.

"A Day of Quality"

HE EASED the car left and down the ramp onto Grand Central Parkway, and in that moment the rear-view mirror filled with the huge, blazing ball of red sun sitting low in the sky behind. He had never seen it quite that way. Turn back and look, quickly, the inner Lucas said, but of course he did not, could not, in the hurtling traffic. Down then, checking the mirrors and looking back over his left shoulder for the moment when he could merge with all the others, at fifty-seven miles an hour in the fifty-mile zone. Once in lane he glanced up at the mirror again, but all he saw was a pink and gray line of clouds. Only a disappearing blush on the parkway signs was left. He felt cheated. A once-in-a-lifetime sunset, and all he had seen of it was what that small mirror could contain, a reflected fragment. Suddenly self-pity ballooned from somewhere inside and surprised him with a brief, fierce moment of resentment.

Ordinarily he enjoyed maneuvering the car in and out of the fast lane, around slower cars. The quick appraisal of traffic behind and to the sides, the decision, the signal, the move, steady or accelerated as the situation required. The feeling of skill in accomplishing it well and safely. But now he stayed in the middle lane and fell back to a sullen, stubborn fifty. Damn us all, he thought, mindless combatants armored in steel and glass and mounted on machines. Where was it he had read that modern man seemed to pursue his sport mainly through his buttocks? Some article about snowmobiling, or maybe motorcycling.

Moving into the darkening east this evening was like driving into a tunnel, especially as he passed under the cantilevers supporting the local road above the parkway. Most times he felt a wholly unreasonable sense of pride at the sight of those cantilevers. He had had nothing to do with them, of course, but the fact that they were there, that human minds had understood that they would work and the physical laws that made them work, filled him with satisfaction simply at being human. This afternoon, abruptly, he hated them, and the ingenuity that had spawned them. Better the quiet roads of fifty years ago, an unhurried and tranquil heart, and a full-faced look at the sunset.

He pushed aside the futility of that line of thinking and tunneled east through the failing light. If the sunset had been the only thing missed that day it might not have hurt so much. But his presentation for the Haldimere account had lost by the slenderest of margins. With it had gone his best hope for a senior partnership. His last glimpse of the carpeted eminence of the twentieth floor was through closing elevator doors. It was gone irretrievably, now and forever, and for the moment, at least, without the peace of an amen. He had castigated himself for the rest of the day, knowing that the presentation had not been right from the start, that he had just not gotten the proper slant, yet blaming pressure and haste for the errors of omission, the faulty planning.

Jacob had said, "Look, Lucas, this isn't helping. You did all right. The decision was made on politics, that's all. Forget it. There'll be other times." Lucas did not believe him and found it difficult even to be grateful.

The expectant lift he usually felt as he bore onto Northern Parkway did not come today. He thought of Sarah, and in advance he resented equally her asking how it had gone, or not asking at all. If she did ask, he would resent her words of consolation, or, oppositely, her silent concern.

This was getting him nowhere. With an effort that seemed to require every muscle of body as well as mind he thought of his schooner model, almost completed. Begun three months ago, after Tom had gotten it for Christmas, it had become his when Tom lost interest. He was on the rigging now, a precise, time-consuming task that occupied his entire being, to the exclusion of every other thought or activity. He had never built a model before, and was continually astonished at the pleasure it gave him.

His mind slipped out of gear again. It was as if someone were in there pulling open file drawers, all the wrong ones, and slamming them shut, but not before the contents partly spilled out and floated to rest in front of his eyes. Under Failures there was his job, twenty years of hard work that had advanced humankind not at all, unless you counted the salary that kept Sarah and the children well cared for. He had been able to say, from time to time, that it was rewarding, it was challenging, and all the clichés that he suspected everyone from clerks to executives used at one time or another. He wondered if he had gone into a profession instead of business things would have been different.

Under Disappointments there was Tom, dreamy, bookish Tom, who seemed unable to alight on even one interest that might lead to accomplishment. He loved him profoundly but would have liked just one small achievement to be proud and paternal about. Instead he had a C student, a middling athlete, a Boy Scout who was unable to master knots. Cheerful always, obliging enough when it came to chores, but nothing for a father to do more than smile at or shake his head over.

Under Frustrations there were all of the things in his life that he needed or wanted to do but probably never could or would get to. Everything from rewiring the house to going around the world on a freighter, which he had dreamed of ever since reading Howard Pease's books when he was a boy. He had never dismissed the hope completely. Before they were married he had asked Sarah if she would go with him when the time came. Her answer had been quick and sturdy. "Sure, Luke. As long as I can be a deckhand. I'd hate to work in the galley."

Remembering brought a measure of contentment, and he managed to get his thoughts under control again. He guided the car into the exit lane and slowed for the stop before turning onto Shore Road.

The car behind him must have been going thirty miles an hour when it hit him. His harness kept him from being flung around or injured, but the unexpectedness of it left him momentarily unable to react. When the other car backed up and rocketed out around him, abrading rubber as it went up over the curb and swung wildly around the corner, he was not even alert enough to be sure of its color. He sat there for a moment, then turned off the ignition, unhooked himself, and got out. Already a long line of cars had stopped behind him. He looked at the back of his car. Rear bumper pushed in, trunk sprung, fenders crumpled. No odor of gas, no sign of a ruptured tank. The driver of the car behind him got out and came up to him.

"Jeez, what a lousy thing to do."

"Yeah." That inadequate acknowledgment, Lucas thought, summed up the whole situation.

"Did you get his license?"

"No. He took off so fast I didn't see a thing."

"I didn't get the number either, but I know it was a late-model Dodge, two-door, blue, small, probably a six-cylinder."

"Thanks. That may help."

"My name's Roy Williams." He fished around in his pockets and came up with a pen and a scrap of paper. "Address and phone number. I'll be a witness if you need one."

"Thanks. I'm Lucas Tyler."

"Let's see if she'll get you home. I'll follow for a couple of blocks."

"Thanks," Lucas said again. The man's matter-of-fact kindness and competence left him feeling absurdly like a helpless child. He got back into his car and cautiously started it. The engine sounded normal, so he made his turn tentatively and started off down the road. There was noisy clattering from the back end, but the car was moving along all right. He heard a horn behind him and looked into the mirror in time to see Williams wave at him and turn off. What a decent guy, he thought.

In the five minutes it took him to reach home Lucas decided that the accident would have one benefit, in that it would distract Sarah from asking about the Haldimere presentation. He was wrong. He clanked into the driveway so loudly that she came flying from the kitchen door, carrying a soapy wet dishcloth, her face working with concern. She wrenched at the door handle before the car had even stopped.

"Good Lord, are you all right?"

"Fine. Darn fool hit me from behind and took off."

Together they went around and looked at the back of the car. She kissed him and said, "It's not so bad, is it? I mean, it's just kind of bashed in."

"A few hundred dollars, I guess. The insurance should cover it, except for the deductible. I've got to call in the accident and make a report."

"I'm just glad you didn't get hurt. How did the presentation go?" So much for distraction.

"We didn't get it."

"Damn." That was all she said. His several scenarios anticipating her reaction had not included this one. All in all, he thought, it was the best.

Tom appeared and looked at the car. "Crimers, Dad, who did that to you?" At first Lucas found it comforting that his son should unhesitatingly attribute the blame to someone else. Then he realized that the question could have been put no other way, since it was highly unlikely that the damage could have been self-inflicted.

"Someone piled into me at the stop sign coming off the parkway."

"Wow, what a mess. I don't see how they'll ever be able to fix it right."

The extent of the damage was in the eye of the beholder, Lucas thought. To Sarah it was merely bashed in, to Tom it looked irreparable, to him it was a matter of indifference so long as the insurance paid for it.

"Where's Libby?"

"Inside, very busy. Even if the car had blown up as you turned in I doubt that it would have gotten through to her."

"What's she doing?"

"It's a surprise. She's working at your desk in the living room, but don't go in there until she sends out word it's all right."

Lucas speculated about the surprise. A four-year-old's creations have rich variety, or at least Libby's did. At home and in his office the walls and shelves and furniture were covered with more or less representational paintings, lumpy pottery, cardboard houses and hats, and cheerful yarn and stick figures.

After he called the police and the insurance agent, he waited in the kitchen with Sarah for permission to enter the living room.

"How about a glass of wine?" she asked. "For a bad day."

"You, too?"

"My day's been all right. It was yours I was thinking of."

He poured the wine and stood by the kitchen counter drinking it, watching Sarah fuss over dinner, letting his mind wander back over the day. The film of distractions that had sealed off his earlier thoughts came unstuck, and again he felt infinitely tired and depressed.

"Libby says it's okay now," Tom called. He took his sister's projects seriously, with not a trace of the derision older brothers sometimes display towards little sisters. He was, in fact, quite in awe of her creativity. Lucas found himself wondering, perversely, if this was normal. Sarah put things straight. "He's a love," she said.

Libby was sitting at Lucas's big desk, her face and hands covered with dabs of white glue and smudges of every watercolor in her paint box. In front of her was a foot-and-a-half square of corrugated cardboard, raggedly cut from a carton. It was painted green, as was a substantial area of the desktop around it. Stuck on it were little painted paper houses, with purple roads and driveways separating them. Tiny bunches of green yarn represented bushes and trees. A wad of brown yarn appeared to be a dog, considerably larger than any of the trees and nearly as large as the houses. There were no people, but one or two houses had windows with faces painted in them. Libby looked at her mother and father anxiously.

"Oh, honey, it's beautiful," Sarah said. "Isn't that beautiful, Luke?"

Lucas searched for a word lavish enough. "Magnificent," he said. "I'm proud of you, Libby."

"Tommy helped, too."

"Not very much." Modesty, or a desire to dissociate himself from the considerable mess on the desktop? Lucas was at once ashamed of his thought. Besides, probably neither of them had even noticed the spilled paint and glue.

The schooner model had been pushed back out of the way. It towered above the little diorama. Lucas was relieved to see that it was unscathed.

They stood around the desk admiring Libby's artwork in its entirety and all of its details until even she tired of it.

"Where shall we put it?" Lucas asked her. "Here on the coffee table where everyone can see it?"

"Oh no, Daddy, I didn't get it good enough for that."

That makes two of us, he thought, who didn't get it good enough today. He said, "Sure you did. Tell you what, we'll talk about where we should put it while we have dinner."

The baked ham was, he guessed, a celebration dinner for the expected success of the Haldimere presentation. He tried for humor: "I'm glad someone brought home the bacon today," at which Sarah made a face and said, "I don't know which is worse, your jokes or the way you're taking this whole thing. One lost contract isn't the end of the world, you know."

"You sound like Jacob. Loyalty is blind and deaf—though certainly not dumb. But thanks anyway." He could not keep the irritation out of his voice.

Sarah put on her I'll-pursue-this-later-when-the-children-aren't-around look, then said, "Bringing home the bacon reminds me of the time in grade school when I got all the way to the state finals in spelling competition. The championship games were held at the capital, and Mother and I went by train and stayed in a hotel. The morning after we arrived I got a telegram from my father and brothers and sisters. It said, 'We know you'll win and bring home the bacon.'"

Tom and Libby asked in unison, "Did you win?"

"Nope. I lost, on a fairly simple word. I felt terrible, not so much for myself as for my mother and father."

"Did you cry?" Libby wanted to know.

"I don't remember for sure, but I don't think so. That isn't the sort of thing you cry about. Now finish up, and while your father and I have coffee you can move your little village onto the coffee table, or wherever you think it'll look best. Then see if you can clean up Daddy's desk."

Lucas expected her to take up the failed presentation again, but instead she said, "I hadn't thought about that spelling contest for years. Funny, how a phrase can set your memory off. That train ride was so exciting, going west into the sunset, all the little villages flashing by. And staying in the hotel, well, that was the grandest thing that had ever happened to me." She smiled at him. "Silly, isn't it?"

"I don't think so. Speaking of sunsets, did you see the one this afternoon?"

"Yes, and it was scary. I don't like that kind; big angry sun turning everything glaring, ugly red. Did you see it?"

"Only in the rear-view mirror, coming onto Grand Central. I wish I could have seen it better."

"You didn't miss much."

They finished their coffee and as he began to help clear away the dishes Tom called him from the living room.

"Just a minute, Tom. I'm helping your mother."

"Please, Dad. Better come now." It was more a command

than a request. Lucas glanced at Sarah, who returned a puzzled look. "That's an S.O.S. if ever I heard one."

Libby was seated at his desk again. Her toy village had been moved. Lying in front of her on its side was the schooner model, toppled over, he guessed, in her efforts to clean the desktop. Libby's small fingers were fumbling with the bottle of glue and the broken masts. Her head was bent but he could see tears spilling slowly, one by one, dropping into the partly completed rigging. Tom was kneeling beside the chair, looking up at her.

It took perhaps a second for Lucas to absorb the whole scene, and as he did he felt the full force of her anguish as if it were his own. It was less bearable than any pain he had ever felt. He picked her up and sat down in the chair, holding her in his lap. Her first sound was a sharply inhaled sob, almost a hiccup, no less terrible for being so small. Then more silent tears, great drops falling on his arm, and finally the storm of grief as he gathered her close and kissed the top of her head.

"It's okay, sweetheart, it's okay. Nothing's worth feeling so bad about. We can fix it. Even if we can't fix it, it's okay."

Tom chimed in. "See, Lib, I knew he wouldn't be mad." He patted Libby's knee and looked up at his father. There was absolute certainty in his eyes, and a small steady smile that stirred Lucas like a benediction. He laid his face against his daughter's hair so that his son would not see, and let the tears spill from his eyes, too.

He insisted that Libby be kept up until her good spirits were fully restored, and all four of them discussed ways to fix the schooner. Then the children went off to bed.

"Well," Lucas said, "it's been a day and a half."

"I know what you mean. This morning seems a year ago. Why don't you fix us a big, wicked drink of something? A stinger, maybe. It's been years since I had a stinger."

"That's because the last time you had such a terrible head the next day."

"I'll only have one this time."

They sat over their drinks for almost an hour, not saying much. Halfway through, Sarah looked over at him. "Tom is so much like you. I hope he never changes." The idea so startled him that he could find no words for a reply. Finally he said, "You really think so?"

"Oh my dear Lucas, yes. Not a bit of ego. Well, hardly any."

He thought it was one of the most sobering things anyone had ever said to him, and he considered it from all sides, carefully, as if she had presented him with some geometric object that required careful examination. First reluctantly and then with growing pleasure he recognized the demonstrable truth she was proposing. "I suppose you're right," he conceded.

Later, as they were getting ready for bed, Sarah said, "It wasn't such a bad day after all. I mean, you lose some, you win some."

"I guess so," Lucas said. "Still, I wish I hadn't missed that sunset."

Postscripts

A Day of Quality

Three small birds exploring the dawn
dispel the night's troubling dreams.

A wave through the neighbor's window
lightens the morning chores.

On the bus a wee child flirts, and
even the weary driver grins.

A power failure dims the office—
untimely (but easing the workload).

Word comes: Beloved friend has died.
Shock shuts down mind and heart.

Lesser adversities go unnoticed
as cheering memories battle grief.

The end of day unfolds slowly
in homely tasks and quiet music.

Three small birds exploring the dusk
slowly reveal perspective:

Joy and sorrow, work and play
fragment the day but leave us whole;
if all mankind could be so blessed.

Scherzo in B-Flat

Remembering Miss Baldwin

The old sheet music—
buried in my piano bench,
worn, but with your penciled marks,
still underlining, cautioning—
erases all the years.

Opening to page three,
tentative fingers find the keys.
How quickly it comes back:
"Lightly now," you say, "make it playful—
that's what scherzo means."

Memory, dimly lit,
recalls the neat brown house,
front parlor with piano,
teacher, waiting with her tiny mother,
to start us on the exercises.

Images drift back—
your commanding presence,
gentle (or unspoken) criticism,
warm words of praise, sometimes,
for our plodding hands.

Behind us, folded deep
in her worn old leather chair,
Mother Baldwin taps her cane—
an unobtrusive metronome,
unseeing but aware.

Is it only she who hears you,
    when you give yourself
    wholly to the waiting keys,
    to Handel, Mozart, Schubert?
    We know only fragments of your skill.

But then at last we hear you
    on Sundays, at the organ.
    Your hands pour forth the music—
    prelude, hymns, and postlude—
    to bury us in worship.

Now memory has composed a trio
    in major/minor keys: firm teacher,
    caring daughter, inspired musician—
    a humble life of joy and duty,
    an opus to aspire to.

Canceled

The Grecian journey, to view
    the marble tributes to the gods;
A time in Rome, and Venice,
    for papal splendor, gondolas;
Adventure in the white-cragged Alps
    to challenge the slopes, then warm at the inn;
A timid look at Africa, to grieve
    the harm his forefathers did;
A voyage to those Asian lands
    where cultures clash in bitter strife.

Instead, the library books returned—
    a slow walk home from the market,
    chatting with neighbors, feeding the dog,
    reading the mail, preparing supper—
    as the afternoon sun fires the clouds,
    then yields to the evening stars.

Credo

Would the world be safer,
    do you suppose,
If those ancient prophets
    in flowing robes
Had refrained from preaching
    their calls to arms,
Advising instead, "live simply,
    do no harm"?

My Dog

Fact is, of course, that she
    is no more mine than I am hers—
and of the two conceits,
    one has only to observe
which of us responds at once
    to the other's call: opening doors,
serving meals, washing feet—
    to know, indeed, that ownership
is at least debatable.
    Fact is, of course, that I am hers.